I0601992

Paperback ISBN: 978-1-64873-496-0
Ebook ISBN: 978-1-64873-497-7

Cover Design, Project Management, and Book Launch
by Writers Publishing House

The Tragic Tale of a Half Breed

Aris Bolvi

1

Throughout the years on earth, the life forms that inhabited it had evolved a lot in their nuclear science to the point where people who had the higher power used it to start wars, many of which destroyed the very ground that they lived on. The residual nuclear waste had tainted the soil and water which had changed fifty percent of the human population's DNA with monstrous traits. Technology was scarce, where only the wealthy were the only ones to possess it. Instead of the normal states in the USA, there were kingdoms; the North Kingdom, the South Kingdom, the East Kingdom, and the West Kingdom. In the middle of the kingdoms was a small unclaimed land that neither of them wanted. It was called Zira.

Zira was a city where all merchants would come far and wide to sell their products. The one attraction that brought most people to Zira was a battle colosseum where the full-blooded demons fought for their lives. On countless occasions, the full-blooded demons reproduced with the remaining humans which created half-breeds. Half breeds were shunned, they were used as slaves, pets, or as bait for the fighters in the battle arena.

Out in the wilderness outside of the borders of Zira, a small eight-year-old girl was out with her siblings learning how to hunt. The girl's name was Shakeera. She was a part of the many half-breeds on earth, she was half human and half cat. Her mother was a cat demon as her father was human. Shakeera looked human but had some characteristics of a cat. She had long brown hair with blue highlights woven within her hair. Perched on top of her head were triangular light brown cat ears with bits of blue fur on them that she hadn't grown into yet. She had big bright blue eyes that were always curiously looking around her. Twitching down at her side was her light brown tail with blue fur that resembled her ears.

Shakeera was looking around her, not paying attention to her sibling's lesson.

"Shakeera!" Her older brother's voice snapped her back to the lesson.

"Yes?" Shakeera squeaked. A teenage boy with spiky brown hair and pointy ears stood there with his hands on his hips.

"Are you paying attention to what I'm trying to teach you here?" He asked sternly. Her ears drooped down as she bowed her head.

"Sorry Mentro...." Shakeera said softly.

"Ok now watch how Knala brings the prey to us." Mentro placed his clawed hand on top of her head. He moved her head so she had to look up to see her older sister was chasing a deer towards them. Knala had brown red hair that curled around her face, her cat ears were flat against her skull as she caught up with the buck. Shakeera's twin sister was sitting beside her squirming with excitement. She looked similar to Shakeera but her hair was darker and her eyes were amber-colored. Her cat ears at little notches were taken off from all the play fights she and her siblings had done.

"Ok Takeera, are you ready? Here's your chance...ready...now!" Mentro ordered. Takeera dashed out of the bushes and ambushed the buck taking it down with no difficulty at all.

Shakeera watched intently until something caught her eye, it was a bright purple butterfly. Her head followed its movement until it had disappeared from view. Silently she snuck away from her siblings to stalk the little insect. She followed it until it landed on a flower bobbing up and down before settling in place. Shakeera sat down next to the flower, her ears forward paying the utmost attention to the beautiful critter. A gust of wind blew disturbing the peaceful moment making the insect take flight. Shakeera lifted a finger hoping that it would land on it. Her eyes grew big as a big smile spread across her face when it fluttered up to her landing on her small finger. Everything seemed so peaceful until a snap of a twig came from behind her making the butterfly fly off. Her brows knitted together in confusion when she looked behind her, three big burly men emerged out of the bushes. Advancing towards her, Shakeera's eyes grew big in fear. She knew who these men were, they were the battle arena's scouts that go and find any unfortunate soul to be bait in the fights.

"Well look what we found here boys, a filthy half-breed kit," One man said.

"Yeah, she's perfect for today's battle. Better grab her before she gets away." The second man said. Shakeera scooted away getting on all fours making a break for it.

"Ah! Mentro! Help me!" Shakeera screamed out just as she was grabbed by the tail by one of the scouts. "Mentro!" She screamed. Off in the distance, Mentro's head turned to the sound of Shakeera's scream.

"Shakeera?" Mentro's eyes widened with fear as his worst nightmare was coming true. He called out to his sisters and ran in the direction where he heard Shakeera's scream.

Shakeera thrashed about clawing and biting at the men that had grabbed her. But nothing she did seemed to deter them. The leader of the group grabbed Shakeera by her ears, roughly making her cry out in pain. The group of men stopped in their steps when they reached their Jeep hearing a mighty roar coming a few yards away. Within five minutes Mentro crashed through the bushes.

"Shakeera!" Mentro called out.

"Mentro!" Help me!" Shakeera called out as the men tossed her into the Jeep and sped off stirring up dust. Mentro raced alongside the Jeep baring his canines at them. He leapt into the air landing on top of the high-speed vehicle and slashing the men in the Jeep with his claws. Mentro attempted to grab Shakeera, but one of the men pulled out a gun shooting Mentro in the shoulder. He called out in pain grabbing his shoulder as they kicked him off the Jeep

"Mentro!" Shakeera cried out as she saw her brother's body disappear in the dust as the Jeep drove away.

One of the scouts pulled a sack over her head knocking her unconscious.

Loud noises woke Shakeera up. Her surroundings were still black due to the sack covering her head. Reaching up she tossed the sack off her head, eyes widened seeing where she was. The place that her mother warned her about since she was born was the Battle Arena.

"If you don't go to bed, little one, the scouts will come and take you away to The Battle Arena." Her mother's voice echoed in her brain.

Looking around her surroundings people were sitting in stands cheering with excitement. They were sitting behind an electric fence for protection. Above the stands was a large black office where the person in charge had the best view of the arena. On top of the office was a large jumbo screen. It turned on reviewing a well-groomed man that looked to be in his mid-forties. He had piercing blue eyes with slicked-back black hair with a stripe of gray on the side of his head. The crowd cheered loudly as they saw him on the screen and the speakers turned on. Shakeera covered her ears as the loud noises hurt her sensitive ears.

"Hello, and welcome to the battle arena! We have a wonderful battle for you today! We found this little half-breed kit at the border. Our hard-working scouts found this poor half-breed alone in the wild. Let's get this battle started, shall we? Here's Bullz Everyone!" The man's voice rang as a siren went off.

Shakeera felt the ground shake as a large door opened up revealing a large Minotaur. He had three long gray horns that were as thick as a tree trunk curling upwards to the sky. His red eyes blazed with power. Steam shot out of his snout as the shiny nose ring jiggled from his movement. A bowling ball-sized spiked ball swung from his tail. Clawing the ground under him, Bullz started his charge towards Shakeera.

2

Shakeera's eyes widened in horror as the large bull creature charged in her direction. The earth shook under her as he grew nearer by the second. Shakeera had no time to think as Bullz had already collided with her, making her skid back barely missing his large horns. Standing up, her knees shook and her heart was beating out her chest. Thinking back to her lessons from her siblings. She remembered that if your opponent is bigger than you, speed is your best weapon. Bullz came back around for another charge attack. Shakeera ran head sliding under him grabbing his tail being mindful of the spikes. Bullz bucked around whipping Shakeera around until he finally flung her into the air. Shakeera screamed as she rocketed into the sky. As she rose above the walls of the battle arena, she saw the landscape that looked beautiful. As she started to descend back down, she noticed that she would be landing right on top of Bullz mighty horns.

Something inside of her, deep inside her, was trying to take over her body. This entity was fighting its way from some box that it was trapped in. Little by little the energy seeped out of this said box which made Shakeera more powerful. The box finally broke open releasing the surge of energy flowing through her veins.

Shakeera's bright blue eyes widened as the energy engulfed her, making her heart pound quicker in her chest. She felt her canines grow longer, her nails grow longer and her hair grow. Her bright blue eyes transformed to a navy-blue color with a demonic look to them. Lunging forward she thrust her claws in front of her, clawing his eyes as she sank her teeth into his snout. Bullz roared in pain, thrashing his head from side to side. After a few minutes, he shook his head hard enough that he flung Shakeera off of him into a nearby wall creating a small crevice. Dust filled the arena obstructing everyone's view of the battle. The dust settled revealing a crater. Inside that crater, a small hand shot out pulling a not-so-happy Shakeera who was baring her fangs. Her eyes were narrowed, her ears flat against her skull. She growled low crawling out of the hole and landed on the ground, her body swaying slightly. The beast stomped his feet, launching himself to a full charge.

With a mind of its own Shakeera's right arm lifted, her palm facing in front of her in the direction of Bullz. Her hand twitched violently as a black hole appeared in the center of her palm. A green vine slithered out like a snake emerging from its home. Red thorns started to grow from the vine glimmering in the sunlight. Just like a gun, it shot out of her palm wrapping around Bullz's foot, making him trip landing flat on his face. Bullz roared in annoyance thrashing about breaking Shakeera's vine. When he broke the vine, another one replaced it. The more he broke the vines the more would appear. Bullz got so frustrated he stampeded towards Shakeera only to have yet another vine shoots out and wrap itself around his nose ring. Pulling herself toward him she landed on top of him. Bullz bucked and thrusted his body trying to get her off his back.

11

After a while, he finally grabbed Shakeera by the leg tossing her off of him. Shakeera smirked as she landed safely on the ground holding on to the vine that was still connected to Bullz's nose ring. Using some kind of unknown power, she yanked the vine so hard, that the nose ring tore right out of his nose. Bullz bellowed in pain grabbing at his nose, he looked up seeing that Shakeera was twirling the medal ring on her finger.

"Probably not the best accessory, you look better without it." Shakeera chuckled.

Bullz's eyes blazed with rage as he prepared for the finishing blow. Just as he jolted forward Shakeera placed her palm flat against the ground. The ground shook as vines shot out from underneath Bullz surrounding him in a green blur. He tried to dodge the attack but to no avail. One by one the vines wrapped around the trashing creature engulfed in a cocoon. The cocoon wiggled every few seconds, the sharp thorns sparkling against the lights overhead. Clenching her fist in the dirt, she dug her claws into the ground and the vines squeezed Bullz like an orange being juiced. His blood pooled under his vined vessel. Shakeera's eyes reverted to her bright blue color. Falling to her knees she grabbed her head in pain. Blinking through the pain she looked around her, seeing Bullz's unrecognizable body lying a few feet away from her, she looked up at the audience. They were silent for a moment then they cheered loudly.

The man in the tower looked down at what had happened in front of him. A sacrificial half-breed that had zero chance of surviving. Pulled a fast one on him and killed his prized battler. He sat there gawking; it took him years to get Bullz to the state he was now just to be crushed. The man clenched his jaw biting the tip of his thumbnail trying to figure out a plan. After panning his sights from the young girl to the audience, he saw how they were reacting to her victory. Then it hit him like a ton of bricks. Releasing his thumb from his mouth, snapping his fingers to summon one of his guards.

"When you captured this girl did you run into any complications?" The man asked.

"Ah, well funny you ask that sir. When we initially grabbed her, a man did try to save her. We believe he was her older brother." One of the guards stated.

"Interesting, did he call out a name by chance?" He asked.

"Let me think, I know she called out his name a lot, Mentro was his name. But, hers was." The guards trailed off tapping his chin.

"Shakeera, I believe was her name." Another guard interrupted.

"Shakeera hmm? She will do nicely in our little family here." The man had a broad grin on his face. He grabbed his microphone, smoothing his hair back.

"There you have its folks! You saw it here, our new champion Shakeera!" The man's voice rang from the speakers.

Shakeera turned her head towards the tower as her name came out of the speakers. She tilted her head in confusion. A gate opened up behind her making her jump in response. Turning around she saw a group of guards approaching

14

her with metal rods with electric sparks shooting from the tops of them. Confusion filled her mind as the guards continued to approach her menacingly, and the audience was cheering happily for her.

"Now, will you cooperate with us or are we going to have to take you by force?" One guard shouted, pushing the electric rod closer to Shakeera's face making her flinch. Shakeera put her hands up in surrender.

"I, I will cooperate. Where are you going to take me?" Shakeera asked, quivering in fear as she got to her feet. The guards walked around her so they were behind her.

"You need to be cleaned off before you go to your cell. Now go! You half-breed!" The guard shouted, jabbing her with the rod sending a wave of electricity through her body.

Shakeera yelped in pain as she stumbled forward. Shakeera was escorted through the gate. Walking down the many twists and turns of hallways they arrived at a large metallic door that automatically opened inward revealing a tiled room that had drains and a variety of bathing utilities. Shakeera was shoved roughly into the room, directing her to the station. People were dressed in white suits with yellow gloves.

"Undress." One of the people ordered pointing at Shakeera.

"Excuse me?" Shakeera questioned; her cheeks flushed.

"I said undress, if you won't do it willingly one of us will not be gentle and undress you ourselves." The person said again with a little annoyance in their voice.

Shakeera swallowed hard as she slowly started to undress in front of all the people in the room. After stepping out of her last garment of clothing, she wrapped her tail around her lower half while using her arms to cover her chest. The person who ordered her to undress made a disgusted noise as they picked up her clothing, placing them in a tub of water. Another person who was dressed in similar clothing pushed Shakeera to the middle of the room instructing her to stay in that spot. She did as she was told.

Looking around the room she saw several people gathering in one area where a metal wheel was on the wall, what looked like a long rubber hose was being pulled in the direction of Shakeera. The man stopped holding the nozzle at Shakeera before pulling the switch, spraying cold water on the small child making her scream in protest. The ice water bit at her skin making her shiver instantly. Shakeera turned away from the hose protecting her body the best she could. The more she turned, the man holding the hose circled her. After what seemed like a lifetime the hose was shut off. Shakeera squatted down shivering violently. Looking up she saw a massive industrial metal fan being wheeled up to her. It turned on making a loud cranking noise as the blades started to rotate. When it got powered up the wind coming from it almost blew Shakeera across the room. The group of people brought her back to the first station to receive her clothing. Just as she put her clothes on the guards had pushed her roughly out of the room and walked her down a stairway of stairs to what looked like a dungeon with barred cells. Shakeera was stopped at a cell with an open door. The guards then placed shackles on both her hands and her feet, pushing her into her cell and making her land face-first onto the stone floor.

As she tried to move her body screamed in protest from the aftermath of the battle. When she tried to move her arms and legs they were weighed down with heavy cuffs and chains bounding her hands and feet together. Tears fell from her eyes. A man walked out from the shadows looking down at her from the other side of the bars of her cell.

"Well, my little half-breed, you did an excellent job today." He praised.

"I...I did?" Shakeera's big ears lifted as she scooted up slightly.

"Does this mean I'm free?" She asked with hope in her voice. The man snickers.

"Far from it my dear. You killed my starfighter. I need a new fighter. You gave everyone a great show out there. You're my new fighter Shakeera, you will fight until you take your last breath." The man stepped back laughing evilly.

Shakeera's eyes watered, her ears dropped down. She looked behind her seeing the full moon's light showing through the barred windows. From that day on Shakeera had fought for her life in that battle arena.

Eight years had passed, Shakeera was now sixteen years old. It was her birthday and the best way to celebrate was to battle for her life once more. It was another free-for-all battle, where several demons showed their strength and tried to take Shakeera's life. This fight was like a walk in the park. No matter what demon that vile man threw at her, she would always win. There were a few close calls here and there where she wasn't paying attention and got severely injured.

There was one contender left, he was a large crocodile demon that was massive in size. His large mouth gaped open with large teeth ready to shred her to bits. Slamming his large tail against the ground, he charged forward snapping his jaws. Shakeera matched his speed with her charging on all fours, ducking under his jaws and tackling his frame making him stagger backward. Locked in their position Shakeera was under him using her strength to keep him standing upright. The crocodile man struggled against her strength snapping his jaws and trying to bite at anything he could get teeth on. Shakeera smirked as she used her tail to tease him. Making it twitch right out of range of his snapping jaws. The crocodile man bellowed in anger, breaking their locked position and pushing Shakeera away. He pivoted and smacked her with his hard scaly tail. Just as his tail made contact with her face Shakeera grabbed onto it, putting him in an awkward position with his head down to the ground with his butt in the air.

The crocodile man then hisses at Shakeera whipping his tail back and forth furiously until he launches her into the air. Shakeera reorients herself looking down at the reptile man with his mouth opened wide revealing his many rows of razor-sharp teeth. Shakeera knew exactly what he was trying to do. Putting her feet under her she landed on top of him with her feet out wide keeping his mouth open.

"Aww, what's wrong? Mouth not big enough to chew your food? Here let me help you " Shakeera taunted as she started to jump on his mouth forcing it to open wider and wider until both Shakeera and the crocodile man were shaking in a power struggle. With one last push from her legs, his jaws came apart. Shakeera stood on top of the crocodile man in triumph. The audience cheered loudly at the battle that had gone on.

"There we have it folks! The birthday girl wins once again. Let's sing her a happy birthday, shall we?" The announcer's voice came from the speakers. The whole stadium was on course with the 'Happy Birthday' song. Shakeera was smiling as she heard them sing to her. The ground started to shake as Shakeera looked up to see a monstrous-sized cat demon claiming over the walls. Shakeera's eyes widened as tears filled them. She knew this cat demon was. It was her mother. The audience started to scream in fear scrambling from their seats to get away.

The cat demon was scanning the area when she finally saw who she was looking for. Shakeera reached out to her mother as more tears poured down her cheeks. Her mother's eyes softened as she climbed down the wall to the ground. Her mother let out a soothing meow as she stepped closer to Shakeera only to get shot at with an electric ball. Shakeera's mother roared in pain looking up at the tower to see a cannon that had just fired at her.

Shakeera whipped her head around to see they were about to shoot another electric ball at her. More guards came into the arena with more weapons. All at once they shot at Shakeera's mother causing her to bleed from her chest. Shakeera's chest grew tight seeing her mother injured because of her.

"Mother! Please leave! I don't want you to die because of me! Please leave and never come back! I love you!" Shakeera screamed, while she whipped her rose vines around violently.

Shakeera's mother looked longingly at Shakeera, tears falling from her own eyes. Turning away Shakeera's mother scrambled up the wall of the battle arena, stopping for a moment to look back to Shakeera then disappearing over the wall. Shakeera lost all control of her legs as she collapsed to her knees.

The usual guards had come to fetch her like her routine was after every fight. Just as they were about to touch her Shakeera snapped her canines at them giving them a warning growl.

"Don't touch me!" Shakeera growled out in rage.

After everything was done Shakeera was sitting in her cell chained up like always. She had a dull look in her eyes, she wasn't all there mentally. When a metal clanking noise drew her out of her zoned-out stage there stood the man in charge looking down at her.

"That was quite a show out there. So? That was your mother huh?" He asked, smirking. Shakeera just sat there giving him all the death glares she could muster.

"Maybe our warning shot might give your family a little insight. To not come here ever again huh? The next time one of your kind comes to bail you out, a warning shot won't be the only thing happening to them if you catch my drift." The man warned as he walked away into the darkness.

3

In the West Kingdom lived a Prince named Alcides. He was betrothed to the Princess of the East kingdom. Both kingdoms were all for this marriage between the two so they could be allies. Alcides on the other hand wanted nothing to do with this marriage. He had no hatred towards the Princess, he respected her like any royal blood would. Alcides just didn't have any romantic feelings for her. He had other things on his mind other than marriage. Tonight, he was planning to leave the castle, to venture outside his parent s kingdom. He felt that something or someone was beckoning for him outside of his castle. Alcides placed his backpack on his bed starting to pack his supplies for his journey.

Alcides had long brown hair that went down to the middle of his back. His skin was a golden brown from all the times he spent outside instead of doing his studies. His honey-colored eyes shimmered in the light from his room as he reached for a map of all the territories. Alcides jumped when he heard a knock coming from his chamber doors.

"Just a minute!" Alcides called out as he chucked his backpack under his bed. He slid on the wooden floor to his desk, grabbed a book, and opened it.

"Come in!" He called, glancing over his shoulder to see it was a maid, Lili. Lili was a sheep half-breed with white golden curly locks with chocolate brown eyes. Alcides's parents assigned Lili to him when they were children so she would be his companion and servant.

"Master Alcides, I brought you the food you requested," Lili said softly. Alcides smiled big, shutting the book with a loud 'flop' noise, and tossed it to the side. He went and grabbed his backpack from under his bed grabbed the food from Lili and placed it in his bag.

"Thank you, Lili. I appreciate you doing this." Alcides stated, placing more items into his backpack. Lili fidgeted with her hands while looking down at her feet.

"Yes, master," Lili said softly.

"Lili what did I tell you, we're equals. We have the same opinions, so just call me Alcides when it's just you and I ok?" He said, looking down at her, and placing his hands on her shoulders. She nodded her head, mumbling her response. Alcides grabbed her hand guiding her to the full-length mirror and handing her a pair of scissors. Lili looked up at him confused as he grabbed a chair and sat down in front of her.

"If I'm going to become a new person, I will have to look the part, right? Well, I need you to cut my hair, I can't do it because I would look like a homeless bum that lost a fight with a mower." He said, drumming his fingers on his lap. In Alcides's family, the men had long hair to show how they were royalty.

"But. Ma...I mean Alcides... I can't just cut your hair..." Lili stumbled on her words. Alcides placed his hands on her trembling ones.

"Please, I don't want to be like the rest of the royal families. I want to be me; I want to walk

my path. Not what my parents planned for me."
He looked at her with pleading eyes.

"Ok..." She couldn't say no to those eyes. She grabbed a comb and proceeded to cut his hair. It only took a few minutes until she said she was done. Standing up he looked himself over in the mirror seeing that he had short shaggy hair. Alcides smiled big turning back to Lili pulling her into a big hug.

"Lili, thank you so much. You have no idea how much this means to me." Alcides released her from his hug to return to his packing. Slinging his backpack over his shoulder walking to the window to see the moon rising over the mountains.

"Now Lili you remember what to do right?"

"Yes, I do." She said softly walking out of his room. A few minutes had passed and a loud crash noise came then a scream that belonged to Lili. He heard the footsteps of the guards and servants going to the noise. Alcides climbed out of his room then started to descend down the lattice panels that were against the castle walls. Stopping at a window he saw Lili was being held by a servant, she opened her eyes and saw him out the window. Alcides winked at her then continued to climb down till he was on the ground. Crouching behind some bushes he snuck his way to the wall that was surrounding the castle. Gripping the stone wall he climbed the high structure until he sat on top seeing the vast forests that lay before him. Glancing behind him he saw the castle that he had lived in his whole life with the glow of the town behind it. Alcide took in a breath and let it out just as he pushed himself off the edge into the darkness of the world beyond the castle.

4

A week had passed and Alcides's food supply was running low. He decided to rest beside a large tree. Figuring out what his next step is going to be. Keep going forward to the next town, or give up and go back home. Alcide looked up seeing the sun sprinkling through the leaves as the wind blew. His eyes started to grow heavy, slowly he blinked and he blinked again when finally, they slid shut. Time seemed to fly by when a snap of a tree branch woke him up with a start. Three silhouettes stood over him, before his eyes could adjust a fist knocked him out cold.

Alcides woke up to the loud sound of cheering. Opening his eyes everything was bright and distorted. After regaining his composure, he finally got to his feet. Looking around he saw he was in the middle of a large arena filled with people cheering from their seats. He was bait for the notorious Battle Arena in Zira, he had heard stories from some of the slaves back home.

"Welcome everyone to the Battle Arena! Today we are having a free-for-all Battle!" The announcer's voice boomed out of the speakers encouraging the audience to cheer louder. Gates from all around him opened up.

"Let's start this fight out with a knockout round, 'catch the piggy'. I present to you the little piggy here, now let's begin!" The voice rang out.

Out of one gate, a snake-like creature slithered out, flicking out its tongue. A giant man came stomping out his hands were large battle axes from another gate. Then lastly a rhino man came stamping out of his gate. The siren went off singling for the fighters to begin.

Alcides stood there in shock, only barely dodging the rhino's charge. Alcides ran as fast as his legs could go. The monsters were battling one another trying to get him. When one was close to getting him, another would knock the other away. As Alcides finally was able to get a few seconds of peace he could hear the audience chant a name.

"Shakeera.... Shakeera..." They spoke.

He was confused about who this Shakeera person was. Was it another monster out to get him? The monsters then stood in front of him stopping their tedious fighting. They started to back him against a wall getting ready to attack.

'This is it...' Alcides thought.

'This is the end.' He shut his eyes tight waiting for his death when he heard a roar like a tiger's. Looking up into the blinding sun to see a black figure jumping from a ledge above him.

A woman landed between him and the monsters. She had long brown hair with bright blue highlights that went to the middle of her back. Light brown with blue fur cat ears perched on top of her head. As he continued to look at her, he noticed that she had a light brown cat tail that twitched in excitement. The crowd cheered the name Shakeera once more.

'This must be Shakeera' he thought to himself. The monsters stood there hesitant to attack, knowing what their fates were going to be, one at a time they charged forward.

"Piece of cake," Shakeera stated. Alcides noticed that a black hole appeared on the hand that was behind her back. Her nails grew longer as a green vine slithered out of the black hole.

The snake creature launched forward. Shakeera grabbed Alcides launching him into the air like it was nothing while thrusting her hand forward shooting the vine out lassoing the snake creature's head. Alcides landed on top of the snake sliding down its back almost colliding with the ax monster but sliding through its legs. The ax monster swung his arms, chopping the snake monster into little bits. Shakeera landed crouched over Alcides; her ears flicked backward. The rhino beast came charging at Shakeera. Kneeling closer to the stunned Alcides, Shakeera placed her hand flat down on the ground. The rhino monster came charging at full speed when a large vine shot up in front of him, making him collide right into it, jamming his horn into the thick vine stock. The rhino creature thrashed about trying to get free but as he jostled about little vines snuck out of the hole that he made and started to wrap themselves around him. Shakeera stood up helping Alcides up. Shakeera only came up to Alcides chest excluding her ears. Shakeera did a pivot turn, her vine slithered up wrapping loosely around Alcides's neck bending him backward as she bent back barely missing being sliced by an ax hand mere inches from their faces. Shakeera got up untangling Alcides from her vine. Shakeera growled with annoyance at the beast.

"Hey! I'd like to have my face on my body! Not like a slice of cheese!" Shakeera yelled at the monster charging after it.

"I will do more than that." The monster retorted back as Shakeera leaped for him to only get backhanded by his blade, sending her soaring into a wall. The audience gasped in surprise. All the commotion went silent as Shakeera was stuck in the wall. The monster stalked over to Alcides. All Alcides could do was stare at the monster wishing Shakeera would come and save him.

"Shakeera," Alcides whispered.

He then heard an explosion coming from behind the monster. Next thing he knew the monster was sent flying into a wall. They're stood Shakeera just as he had hoped. But something seemed different about her, her appearance was different. Her hair was longer whipping wildly behind her. Her usual blue eyes were navy blue with a demonic hue to them. Large canines protruded from her lips and her nails were longer. The vine that was coming from her hand was thicker with bigger thorns that dripped a liquid that when it landed on the ground dissolved then ground.

The monster got up letting out an earth-shaking roar charging Shakeera at full speed. Alcides watched in horror as the monster ran but for a split second there were two boys one with brown hair with steel blue eyes and the other with black hair and multi-colored eyes wrestling on the ground. Just as they had appeared they disappeared right when the monster stomped through where they had appeared. Shakeera whipped her thorned vine around her wildly then tossed it out like a fishing pole letting the vine wrap the ax monster up like a mummy. Lifting the monster into the air slowly she started to constrict the monster like a python. The more the monster struggled, the tighter the hold would get. As he started to grow tired from the constriction Shakeera gripped the vine with both hands ripping the vine into two. When the ripped vine came in contact with the mummified monster, its body was ripped into shreds. Bits and pieces of its body fell from the sky, blood splattered everywhere coating the surrounding area in red. In a flash Shakeera was behind Alcides, her sharp claws pressed against his throat threateningly.

"I want him as my prisoner!" Shakeera called out. The audience cheered as the announcer's voice came from the speakers.

"You've seen it here folks, the best from our one and only Shakeera! Just as she has requested, she will have her new little toy and a nice rest. Until next time." The announcer's voice rang.

Guards came up to Shakeera surrounding her and Alcides with the shocking rods. After shocking her a few times she reluctantly let go of

Alcides. They put shackles and chains on her and a muzzle. Other guards came up to Alcides grabbing him, taking him in a separate direction where they were taking Shakeera.

5

Alcides was escorted through a gate and the noise of the audience grew quieter as he walked through the hallways. The guards stopped at a large double door that had a large sign with the name Chase Scott engraved into it. The doors opened revealing a large office that had an overview of the arena. A large dark red velvet couch sat in the middle of the large window. There stood a man with his back to Alcides. The man threw his hand in the air laughing loudly as he turned around walking towards Alcides.

"There he is! The man of the hour!" The man waved the guards away and wrapped his arm around Alcides's shoulders walking with him up to a large table with an assortment of foods and drinks.

"You must be dying of thirst, my boy! Please help yourself to anything you want!" Alcides dived right into the iced water. Gulping it down quickly. Next, he went to the mini sliders and finger foods.

"You did a great job out there surviving with all those monsters that wanted nothing more than to just kill you with no remorse. She must see something in you if she wants to keep you around." Alcides stopped stuffing his face mid bite looking at the man.

"My name is Chase Scott; I am the founder of this establishment. Do you know anything about the battle arena, uhh what's your name?"

"Uhh it's Alcides." Alcides said, wiping his mouth with his sleeve.

"And no, I don't know anything about what you're doing here." Alcides waved his arm in front of him.

"Well, Alcides, let me give you a history lesson here. Show you what I am doing here." Chase placed his hand on Alcide's back guiding him back to the hallway.

"In this day and age people are so worried that they won't see the sun the next day with all these bad monsters out and about. They work to survive to provide for their family. I want to help ease everyone's minds, help them with their stressful life's. I entertain them by weeding out all the pumped testosterone filled monsters." Chase stated as they continued to walk through the long hall. Alcides glanced out the windows to see the cleanup crew clearing out the battle arena of the previous battle's mess.

They continued walking down the hall until there was a fork in the road, the path split into two. The hall turned into a white path as the one on the left turned into a golden color with an array of arrangements of flowers. Chase led Alcides down the white hallway. As they continued walking Alcides heard the echoes of male's voices shouting and what sounded like water being sprayed. Chase had stopped at a large window that overlooked a tiled room with drains everywhere. Alcides peered into the window seeing Shakeera walking into the room. More like being let to slaughter that is with the guards jabbing her with the electric prods. Shakeera stopped at a clothesline disrobing with her back to the guards. Bit by bit Shakeera took off her clothing revealing her dirty bruised up body with a handful of wounds all along her body. After she pinned her clothing to the clothesline, she used her tail to cover as much as her private parts the best she could as she walked the walk of shame towards the middle of the room. Two guards walked up with two large hoses aiming them at Shakeera.

"As you can see this is a very masculine sport, Alcides. But one day little Shakeera here was in the same shoes you were. But since she is born a half breed the world has already chosen her fate. Just as I did to you, I threw her into the battle for her life. Something in that little girl that day resonated and she killed my top fighter. So, I took her in and trained her to be the killer that she is now." Chase gestures to Shakeera who was being sprayed by both of the men's hoses, all of the blood and dirt dripped off of her going into the drain.

One of the guards pointed their hoses to her dirty clothing on the clothesline and started to rinse them off. Shakeera knelt down covering most of her body so she could wash her hair in the process. Once Shakeera was done getting cleaned some men came up dressed in all white handing Shakeera a loose-fitting gown.

"What are they doing now?" Alcides asked while Shakeera was being escorted back to the hallway.

"As I have told you before this is a masculine sport, which means males are the usual competitors. When the winners of the battle are done fighting, they get to have their special prize at the end. They get cleaned up just as you have seen here and get escorted to our beauties." Chase guided Alcides back into the hallway following Shakeera from a distance. They walked down the golden hallway where everything was beautifully designed with flowers and other feminine decor.

"Beauties?" Alcides questioned.

Further down the hallway there was a large red door with roses carved into the door frame. A faint smell of incense could be smelled coming from it. The doors opened up revealing a fully furnished room with a large bed. On all four corners of the bed goldenrods went up to a canopy that overflowed with dark red curtains. Around the room were tables of exquisite foods and drinks. Four women walked out of the room to the hallway wearing very revealing lingerie that was very pleasing to the eye. Once they saw who the winner was their faces turned pink with the excitement of what was about to happen. They walked up to Shakeera who looked pleased to see them as well. There was one woman who was a human, Shakeera kissed her on the lips while tracing her jawline. Two of the women were half breed rabbit girls, one had one brown ear that stood up while the other was bent in the middle while the other had black ears that were bent in the middle. Shakeera ran her clawed hand through their soft multi-colored hair cupping the back of their heads drawing them in closer. She nuzzled the one on her left while kissing from their temple down the jaw making her way to her neck nipping it softly. Turning to her right she did the same to the other bunny girl. The fourth woman walked up who was a full-blooded female lizard. Her scales were a blue green color, when the light hit it the right way little rainbows appeared. Her under belly was a light blue color. She wrapped her arms around Shakeera who ran her claws along the lizard girl's back strumming against her scales. The lizard girl's tail slithered up and wrapped around Shakeera's tail.

"The winner usually request's what kind of beauties they want. Shakeera here has quite a unique taste in beauties." Chase said as a feminine male who was also dressed like the other girls came out walking up to Shakeera kneeling down before kissing her belly.

Shakeera smirked, running her clawed hand through his wavy locks grabbing the back of his head pulling him up so they shared a steamy kiss ending it with Shakeera biting his bottom lip drawing it back with her teeth letting it pop out. Shakeera walked into the room with her beauties in tow. The doors closed with a soft click; moans soon came echoing through the halls. Chase then escorted Alcides back through the hall to the room they were in for the first time.

"Will Shakeera ever be let go? Will she ever be free from all this?" Alcides asked, grabbing more to eat and drink.

"Oh, she will be, once she breathes her last breath in this battle arena will she be free. If I let her go now, she wouldn't have it as good as she does here. Out there she will end up being someone's pet, or slave. She's programmed to be here Alcides, there is no changing her." Chase said right before taking a sip of his wine.

An hour had passed. Chase got up and escorted Alcides out of his office proceeding down the hall to the two-way split. They took a turn to the right walking past the shower chamber. They came to a staircase leading down deeper into the facility. Walking through the bricked hallway that was lit by torches there were cells lined up on either side of the room with iron bars. They had stopped at a large cell at the far end of the room. In the corner of that room was a makeshift bed made out of straw and ripped up clothes. At the other end was a rusted up manmade toilet that looked like it was about to break. Between those was a barred window that showed the view of the surrounding outside area. A guard walked up to Alcides handing him a wrapped package that contained raw meat that had already started to seep through the bottom. Chase gently pushed Alcides into the cell, closing it loudly behind him.

"Well, Alcides, my brother, this will be your new home. It was a blast talking with you, sorry that this is the last place you will ever see." Chase said with his arms behind his back starting to walk away.

"Wait, what do you mean my last place?" Alcides turned around watching Chase walk away. Chase then nodded his head behind him. Alcides glanced to his side seeing a skeleton leaning against the wall by the bars.

"Why don't you ask the last guy Shakeera brought back with her." Chase chuckled.

Then minutes passed as the sound of chains being dragged echoed through the halls. Alcides leaned forward peering through the bars seeing shadows of people walking down the staircase. Two guards with electric rods walked through then someone who was hunched over dragging their chains on the floor then two more guards followed behind. The group stopped at the cell that Alcides was occupying. They opened the door stepping to the side revealing Shakeera who was muzzled like a savage animal, her arms were cuffed in front of her as her feet were chained in cuffs. Shakeera shifted her feet walking slowly into the cell turning towards the guards giving them a warning growl making them leave. Alcides stood there by the window watching Shakeera walking to her makeshift bed and plop down with an annoyed huff. Alcides looked at Shakeera then back at the packaged meat in his hand.

"Uhm…would you like to eat this?" Alcides stepped forward offering the package. Shakeera looked at the package then back to her cuffed hands.

"You know I would love to eat that meat if I was able to get these damn shackles and cuffs off." Shakeera said in a sarcastic voice tilting her head to the side, eyes narrowed.

"But it takes one other person to push the release switches and normally it takes a couple of days until the guards remember to come back. Whatever meat they give me is usually rotten by the time I get to it." Shakeera added, presenting her cuffed hands.

"Oh...oh! Right, umm sorry here let me try to help you." Alcides scrambled to kneel in front of her trying to make heads or tails of the mechanism that bound her limbs together. Alcides shifted his eyes back to Shakeera who was staring at him intently, her blue eyes not shifting or blinking.

Whenever Alcides would bring his hands near the sides of her face her ears would shift so they tilted back then returned forward when he removed his hands. He quickly took the muzzle off then returned back to the shackles. After a minute passed, he found the two switches on either side of her cuffs and shackles switching them to the offsetting making them fall to the ground with a loud clank. Shakeera rubbed her wrists then her ankles revealing the scars and bruises that appeared.

"Oh, here's the meat you wanted." Alcides handed her the package. She snatched it up quickly, tossing the paper aside, scarfing the meat in mere seconds. After she ate the meat, she started to lick her hand and fingers like a cat grooming itself. Alcides sat there shifting his eyes between Shakeera and the skeleton. Shakeera huffed, rolling her eyes before speaking.

"Before you start accusing me of things. Unlike the guard's tall tale, no, I did not kill that kid. Yes, I did eat him after he passed. There was not much of a burial for whoever ends up here." Shakeera said with no emotion. A part of Alcides knew she wouldn't have killed anyone when not provoked. She's not a savage animal.

"What happened if you don't mind me asking?" Alcide asked.

"Just like how you and I got thrown in, a half breed fox boy was bait for a battle one day. I felt bad for him because I knew he wouldn't have survived like I did. So, I took him in. It happened after I saved him. Before the battle had ended, these big rocks for brain muscle guy had grabbed the kid by his tail and flung him into a large boulder. In result he had a pretty bad head injury, didn't think much of it because he jumped right back up. After the battle I helped him clean his wound and such. I felt like he was my own kit. The blood stopped coming out after the wash but the back of his head felt sponge like. I assumed that it was just the trauma from the battle and that it would go down with some rest. After a while he couldn't talk in fluent sentences, his body started to shut down from his legs to his arms. Then one day after I came back from another battle to find him sitting in his own piss. His eyes were bugged out and looking in opposite directions." She demonstrated by putting her index fingers out pushing them away from each other. "When I came up to him knowing he was slipping. He barely could register that I was there. He mumbled one word as he let out his last breath. 'Mom' He went limp as that one word left his mouth." Alcides's chest grew tight, his heart strained from the story he heard.

"After about a day insects start to infest his body. The guards wouldn't do anything but bad mouth the little boy. I started to eat his body as the guards gawked at me saying how much of a beast I was. I left what was left of his body in that corner so that everyone can see what happened with that little half breed boy." Shakeera said, looking at the skeleton with such sadness in her eyes.

"I'm sorry you had to go through such a difficult situation." Alcides said softly.

"Have you tried to escape from this place?" Shakeera looked at him like he was stupid.

"Hmm let me think." She looked at her arm counting two scars on her arm then pulled up her shirt revealing a large scar on her side right under her breast.

"Ah. yeah, I get it now." Alcides concluded

"There was one time that my mother tried to save me though. I was sixteen and it was a night spotlight fight. My mother is a demon cat,

51

my father is human. As I was in a tussle my mother in her beast form comes bounding into the Arena to come save me. Like ants to a piece of candy all the guards came swarming out at bombarded her with those damn shocking rods and other weapons. She tried to grab me and escape but as she was about to leap out, Chase had this new contraption he only used on the wildest of monsters. He shot her in the eye making her drop me and save herself. I understood this, I told her to leave. That I loved her and that someday we would see either other again someday." Shakeera's voice wavered as tears threatened to fall. She sniffed rubbing her nose and cleared her throat.

"Hmm, there has to be a way to get out of here without getting hurt and or killed." Alcides tapped his chin, racking his brain for some kind of idea. A noise from above drew their attention to the barred window above them.

"Psst! Shakeera! You there?" A female voice whispered through the bars.

"Takeera? Is that you? Thought I told you not to come here anymore." Shakeera growled low standing up grabbing the bars pulling herself up.

Alcides looked up to see a figure wearing a hooded cape. The figure pulled the hood back revealing a girl that looked identical to Shakeera but she had amber colored eyes. Her hair was light brown with dark blue highlights and her ears had little notches of her ears taken off.

"I know but I can't just stay home knowing you're locked up here against your will." Takeera said, grabbing the bars next to Shakeera's. Takeera's eyes glanced behind Shakeera seeing Alcides.

"Sis who's that? Not another bait that you saved, is it? You remember the last time you tried saving someone." Takeera warned

"This is...uhh...I didn't catch your name." Shakeera turned her head back glancing back at Alcides.

"My name is Alcides."

"Alcides here isn't like the kid he is stronger than him, now back to what I was saying. What are you doing here, do you want to end up injured like mom?" Shakeera's ears flicked back.

"I'm good at blending in, you know this. Mom still wants to save you; she just didn't expect so many fancy weapons. I haven't given up yet sis. I will get you out of here one way or another. I will get you out of this death trap. Just stay alive a little longer sis I love you." Takeera leaned forward slightly, nuzzling her nose through the bars against Shakeera's. Pulling the hood back over her head she ran off into the night. Shakeera hopped back down, sighing loudly as she sat down on her bed.

"That sister of mine I tell you; she is as stubborn as I am. We get that from our mother. Takeera is my twin sister, she's been coming to check on me ever since I got trapped here. But I keep telling her that there isn't any way to get out of here. The guards only come to get me when it's battle time or if I'm sick or injured."

"That's it!" Alcides exclaimed, pounding his fist on his palm.

"What's it?" Shakeera jumped in surprise.

54

"You know your way around here, right?"

"Like that's even a question. I've been here since I was eight. I know this place like the back of my hand."

"Ok here's what my plan is." Alcides lowered his voice leaning in closer to Shakeera. She huddled close to him.

"Ok so here's the plan. We make it look like you got injured from your last fight. You were fighting a snake monster, right?"

"Yeah?"

"Well, we can make a fake wound on you, then I call for help and the guards come in to check on you and when they get close enough you attack them."

"That may work let's see." Shakeera started to sniff around then she sniffed Alcides then pulled back.

"Ok so I smell some leafy greens that are still in your pocket and some blueberries." She pointed at his pocket. Alcides reached into his pocket pulling out some salad leaves with two blue berries. Shakeera reached into her shirt pulling out some small strawberries.

"Go grab me a small piece of bone or something that has a small point at the end." Shakeera instructed.

Alcides got up looking around the cell that had bones scattered around. He found a small bone that looked like it was snapped in half with a sizable pointy part. Alcides returned back to Shakeera who was rubbing the lettuce along her neck turning her skin green. Squishing the blueberries between her fingers she rubbed the blue juice under her eyelids and long her lips. Alcides handed her the bone and watched her poke the strawberry with the pointy part.

"Now make it look like I got a snake bite and that the poison is spreading."

"Ok, I'll do my best." Alcides said getting the tip of the bone shard red from the strawberry. Shakeera shifted her position so she was sitting cross legged facing him with her head turned to the side. Alcide leaned forward making little poking gestures against her neck making two little red dots like a snake bite, then he proceeded to make squiggle lines around the wound and down her neck.

"There I think this will do." Alcides said, sitting back looking at his handy work.

"Ok, let me get into position." Shakeera got up spinning around on one foot then fell to the ground on her back arms sprawled out one above her head then the other out to her side. Shakeera closed her eyes, her mouth opened slightly like she was in agony. Alcides walked up to the bars of the cell grabbing a bone from the ground taking a big breath then started to slam the bone against the bars then started screaming.

"Guards! Hello! Someone helps! She's been poisoned.!" Alcides exclaimed. Two guards eventually came after fifteen minutes.

"What's going on here?" One guard asked.

"She was bitten by that snake monster from the battle today. I think she's dead." Alcides pointed at the supposed dead Shakeera.

"I didn't see a bite on her when we bathed her, did you?" One guard asked the other guard.

"No, I didn't see any, at least I thought I didn't see any." The second guard scratched his head, his cheeks flushed.

"You weren't even paying attention, were you? You got distracted by her body again didn't you!" The first guard smacked the second guard's head.

"Well, we better check or we will be the one's really dead. You, prisoner, stand over there with your hands above your head." The first guard ordered Alcides.

Alcides walked to the other side of the cell putting his hands above his head. The first guard came up to Shakeera, poking her with the bottom of his shocking rod. She didn't budge. He knelt down examining Shakeera moving her head from one side to the other. He then noticed the 'bite wound' and hissed in disgust. "Oh god, that's nasty. It stinks too!" The guard made a gagging noise. Shakeera's eyebrow twitched. He bent down closer looking at the infected area, just as he was about to touch it Shakeera's eyes flashed open.

"You don't smell the ripest either." She stated as she locked her legs around his neck lifting him up in the air spinning on her hands snapping his neck while twisting her legs making his head face the opposite direction. Alcides came up to the other guard, shanking him in the neck with the serrated bone.

"Come on, let's go!" Alcide exclaimed.

"Follow me, I know where to go." Shakeera took off running through the halls as Alcides try to keep up. Shakeera stopped at a wooden door that was labeled 'Winner's keeps' Shakeera used the keys that the guards had and unlocked it revealing a room filled with gold and other valuables.

"What is this?" Alcides asked in awe.

"This is the winnings from all the fights I fought throughout the years. Whoever bets against me and I win I get whatever they bet against me. Gold, jewels, even fine lining." She said while grabbing some robes and wraps disgusting herself. Grabbing some pouches she put some gold pieces and some jewels in them, flinging them to Alcides.

"We're going to need this for our trip."

She wrapped a scarf around her head tucking in her ears. Alcides and Shakeera snuck through the tunnels until they came to the back exit of the battle arena. There were two guards standing watch. The two guards talked amongst themselves saying it was time for a change of shift. They started walking towards Shakeera and Alcides who were hiding in the shadows. As the guards walked past and disappeared down the hall Shakeera and Alcides ran for their lives to a building far from the Battle arena. After making it safely Shakeera looked behind her seeing the large lights shining in the night sky attracting the many onlookers to it like a moth to a flame. Ten long years Shakeera's been living in that place now she is free.

6

Shakeera glanced over at Alcides who was grabbing the front of his shirt tightly. She tilted her head to the side, placing a hand on his arm. He jumped slightly looking at her with eyes full of stars. His face had a bright refreshed look.

"That was so rejuvenating! I have never done anything like that before." Alcides beamed with excitement.

"What? Have you never killed a person or been stealthy enough to escape?"

"Yes, to all of that. Back at my kin...my place there wasn't anything fun like this. Only somewhat fun thing was training with mannequins on spinners. The way you fight, man, your style is amazing." Alcides turned to her, staring into her eyes. Shakeera stiffened up, blushing from embarrassment.

"Ah, well it's nothing really. I just learned a lot of it from my older brother and sister before I got captured."

"Your family must be really amazing living out in the wilderness and such."

"Yeah, it was hard but we made it through."

"Alright let's get some supplies for our trip." Alcides said, standing up offering Shakeera his hand.

"Our trip?" Shakeera grabbed onto his hand being pulled up.

"Yeah, I'm going to take you to a better place than this."

"I would rather go find my family."

"Sure, after I take you to my place, I want you to be treated like a normal person and not an animal. You at least deserve that."

"That's true." Shakeera said uncertainty.

The pair started walking away from the battle arena to the notorious market place in Zira. All sorts of people came to this market place, and a lot of vendors set up shop there. But after the sun goes down the whole atmosphere changes from what it was when the sun was up. The red and orange glow from the lanterns draws you in. The scent of incense and other intoxicating smells fills your senses. The music that was played had a deep rhythm that made your body sway to the drum beat. As Alcides and Shakeera walked past the stalls Shakeera noticed that there were some businesses that glowed a dark red with dark figures on stages moving rhythmically to the music that was being played.

Alcides couldn't even imagine what people were selling in this market. It consisted from live half breeds being sold as slaves, to pottery and food. It was endless here but Alcides had to remind himself that he didn't have time to doddle around; he had to get Shakeera out of here before anyone else noticed. He first stopped at a stall that was selling water pouches, after a few minutes of trying to get the merchant's attention he bought a couple for him and Shakeera. The next stand he went to was one that was selling a variety of weapons. All sorts of swords, and clubs. There were whips with spikes on them assortment of guns and shocking prods. What really caught his eye was a jagged blade that had leather wraps around the handle. The next stall they came to was a stall that sold non-perishable foods for people who travel.

"Welcome, what can I help you with?" An older man with a bushy mustache greeted them.

"Hello! We need some food for our travels to the west." Alcides stated.

"Ah yes, why is a young couple like yourself traveling west?" The man glanced between Alcides and Shakeera.

Alcides wrapped his arm around Shakeera's waist pulling her close to him.

"My wife, and I are eloping to my village and we don't really have the money for transportation so we are just gathering supplies for our trip." Alcides beamed. He felt Shakeera grow stiff then grabbed the side of his shirt.

"Oh, eloping you say? Why are you doing that if you don't mind me asking?"

"My father..." Shakeera stated softly looking up at the old man pulling back her hood revealing her cat ears then pulled it back down pretending to get teary eyed. "My father is ashamed that I am a half-breed but my darling husband is here." Shakeera gripped his shirt tightly looking up at Alcides.

"Promised me that we would be happier in his village." Shakeera sniffled burying her face into his chest.

"Oh, my dear girl, I know how all that is. My wife is a half-bred and we had to go through that too. Here let me get your items for you on the house." The old man proceeded to grab a variety of foods, putting them in a sack.

"Really? Thank you sooo much mister." Shakeera beamed at him. Alcides knew he was pushing his luck with the whole wife thing, but her acting was pretty on point. The man came back with a big bag of supplies. Just as Alcides grabbed the sack the battle arena lights flashed on and alarms started to go off.

"Well thank you again sir but we have to head out now, you know our long journey and all. Have a good day!" Alcides exclaimed while grabbing Shakeera's hand taking off through the crowd of people in the market.

Alcides weaved through the crowd, making more distance from them and the battle arena. Shakeera followed Alcides the best she could when something caught her eye. There was a teenage girl sitting on a rug that had a few trinkets. In her arms she held a baby that looked like a half-bred that was malnutrition. Shakeera stopped in her tracks yanking Alcides to the ground. Alcides sat up glancing over seeing Shakeera take off her robe and rolling it up neatly walking up to the teen. Shakeera knelt down in front of the young woman handing her the clothing. The teen shook her head saying she couldn't take them. Shakeera insisted on it petting the young baby's head. Shakeera got up and returned to Alcides who was standing there with a smile on his face.

"Why did you give her your winnings?"

"She would have better use of it then me. She could sell it to feed her starving baby." She said looking back at the girl. Shakeera and

Alcides walked to the entrance of Zira stopping for a moment to look behind them at the vast bounty of this place. The battle arena loomed behind the marketplace like an ominous dark figure. Shakeera walked off the path to the forest turning slightly back looking back at Alcides, her tail swaying behind her. "Well, 'husband' since you want me to see your village so bad show me the way." She gestures into the vast forest. Alcides's face burned from the word husband. Rolling his shoulders back he walked into the forest starting the long journey back home.

7

Alcides and Shakeera walked through the woods for two days and the tension between the two started to grow thin. Alcides wasn't too confident in his leading skills and Shakeera sensed it.

"We're lost, aren't we?" Shakeera broke the silence.

"I...uhh...yes...these surroundings don't look familiar." Alcides looked around thoughtfully.

Shakeera dragged her hand down her face in frustration. She started to walk around looking at trees. Placing her hands on her hips she clicked her tongue then stomped her foot.

"What's wrong?" Alcides asked looking at her weird.

"We've been walking in circles." Shakeera continued as she walked up to a tree showing claw marks etched in the bark.

"The first day we set out I clawed up this tree to track where we were going."

"Really? What? What's wrong" Alcides asked looking at Shakeera who had her ears flicked back and her tail was low twitching at the end.

"Someone or something's hunting us." Shakeera lowered her voice hunching down like she was on the prowl.

Alcides looked around his surroundings not seeing something but suddenly feeling like someone was behind him. Whipping around he peered into the forest not seeing anything different at first. But after looking a few seconds he started to see floating eyes.

"Lost, there's something over here..." Alcides called out to Shakeera pointing in front of him. Shakeera turned her attention to where Alcides was pointing at. She saw something shiny coming from one of the bushes that looked like a pipe.

"Hey! Look out!" Shakeera called out running towards Alcides. Throwing her hand out she wrapped her vine around his neck pulling him back just before a dart came whooshing past his head. Shakeera stood in front of Alcides prepared to fight.

"What are those things?" Alcides asked, standing behind her using her as a shield.

"From the looks of it they are peacock people, I've fought one of their kind at the battle arena. All I know is that the males use their tails as a distraction before they attack. I don't know much about them other then what I dealt with." Shakeera stated.

'Pathoot'

A dart shot out; Shakeera blocked it with her arm. Shakeera hissed pulling it out then tossed it to the ground.

"What was that?" Alcides asked, looking at her arm seeing it had a light shade of purple on it.

70

"It's their paralyzing darts. It's made by the parzberry. The berry has a paralyzing effect to whoever eats it. I grew a tolerance to it as a kid so I should be fine. But a normal human like you would get knocked out by one dart. Just don't look at the floating eyes, they have a hypnotic power about them." Shakeera glanced behind her to see that Alcides had a vacant look in his eyes.

"Too late..." Shakeera turned her attention back to the situation at hand. Baring her fangs hunching forward letting out a warning hiss. A few more darts came flying at her hitting their target. A bombardment of darts flew at her making her look like a life size pincushion. Her body started to sway from all the poison in her body. Placing her hand on the side of her face she could feel the effects of the poison. Something was different though; her brain was feeling hazy. Her eyes started to dilate and her world started to spin. She looked at her hands that were covered in darts but they looked warped.

"What the hell...did they put in these darts..." Shakeera slurred, falling to her knees.

"Catnip" A female voice stated.

"Shhht" Shakeera fell to her side trying to wave away whatever was in-front of her.

Alcides woke up startled, looking around him seeing he was in a hut. Next to him Shakeera was laying on her back, her arms outstretched in every direction.

"Shakeera? Hey Shakeera you, ok?" Alcides asked, shaking her lightly. Shakeera just mumbled about something scratching her belly then rolled over to her side.

"Oh, good you're awake." A female's voice came from the doorway. Alcide looked up to see a woman that had brown slick back hair with speckled green along the roots. A single stem of hair curled up that had a blue green eye on it. She wore what looked like a brown petticoat with a white under shirt with black pants.

"Who are you? What do you want from us?" Alcides asked, placing an arm over Shakeera.

"Don't worry we aren't here to hurt you or your mate." The female started smiling.

"My name is Arsena. I want to welcome you both to our colony." Alcides blushed at the term mate but glanced around the room seeing that there isn't anything threatening.

"Your colony?" Alcides asked.

"Yes, our colony is the Peaconian's. We are peacock demons." Arsena stated, walking up to the bed.

"So why did you drug us?" Alcides asked.

"Well at first, we thought you were an intruder but after we saw who your companion was, we just took you all in and healed you. We didn't know she was our savior."

"Savior?"

"Years ago, we had a bad person in our community that was trying to turn our community into a bad one so we had him go to the battle arena and prove himself. When we caught wind that he was eliminated by her hands, we were beyond grateful.

"I do recall Shakeera talking about fighting someone like you."

"Yeah...I did say that." Shakeera groaned, sitting up in bed holding her head.

"Shakeera how are you feeling?" Alcides turned to her.

"Yeah, just had a little too much...whatever you put in those darts..." Shakeera waved her hand towards Arsena.

"My apologies Miss Shakeera, we didn't know who you were at the time. It took a lot of our paralyzing darts to take you down. We didn't think the catnip infused darts would be the trick to take you down." Arsena bowed her head.

"It's ok, don't worry about it. I was surprised I was able to withstand that much anyway. So that bird for brains guy I battled while back was from your colony? He sure was hellbent on getting rid of females huh? He squawked about being inferior and what not."

"Yes, his thoughts on how our partnerships coordinate was not right. The males use their tails to distract the prey while we the females attack while the prey is hypnotized. He believes that the females should be subordinate and wait on the

74

male's hand and foot. We believe that the males and females are a team that we work together " Arsena stated.

"Huh, that kinda reminds me of how lions work." Alcides tapped his chin.

"Well in my line of work as you know, I'm forced to fend for myself with no one else to help me. So even if you're a male or female you just fight to live. Everyone is out to get you no matter what they say. You have to be a full breed to get special treatment. When you're a minority you're just tossed out for the wolfs." Shakeera's face grew tense.

"Oh no, that's not how it is at all. I'm sorry that you had to go through that. The way you want your life to be is how you make it to be. It shouldn't matter how much of a full, or half breed you are. Do you want to be known as Shakeera and her tragic tale of a half breed? Or do you want to be known as Shakeera that mighty warrior that survived hell and back? Against all odds, you single handed beat anyone that was thrown at you." Arsena punched the air above her head.

Shakeera's ears flicked forward her tail twitching with excitement.

"Now if the both of you are feeling up for it come join us in our celebration?"

"Celebration? Of what?" Alcides asked.

"Well, celebration of the time we rid of that bad person. Come! Let's join the others." Arsena pulled the curtain back letting in the setting sun.

Shakeera and Alcides stepped out of the hut to see the village was bustling with life. The males of the Peaconians stood tall with their long necks, their noses in the air as the sun reflected off their multi-colored plumage. They wore what looked like a green jacket that was made out of feathers. At the end of their jacket was an array of long feathers that had rows of blue eyes they went from small to a large blue eye. A male walked up to the group bowing his head slightly as he nuzzled Arsena affectionately.

"Hello Arsena my darling. I see that our new friends are awake. My name is Zeek. I am Arsena's mate and she is mine forever!" Zeek announced throwing his head back letting out a loud caw that rang to the heavens as he made a shimmy motion with his shoulders fanning out his tail feathers. When Zeek did his call other males did theirs as well mimicking his display by fanning out their tail feathers.

"Oh, now Zeek, you're going to rally the whole village up." Arsena waved her hand at him. Zeek chuckled lowering his plumage.

"I know I know, but I always have to take the opportunity to proclaim my loyalty to my mate. Now Shakeera, if you would do us the honor and participate in our first activity?" Zeek started to walk through the village.

"What activity is that?" Shakeera followed.

"We have a fun thing we like to do; we bring in our toughest villagers and have them spar showing their strength. Since you were the one that took down Trent's in your battle arena why not demonstrate your strength." Zeek stopped at a wooden circular corral.

"But there is only one rule. We don't fight to the death here; we just fight till someone submits."

"Alright, no killing, no problem." Shakeera cracked her knuckles hopping over the wooden fence.

It was a good size area, with wooden stands that wrapped around the area. Zeek let out a loud call that got everyone in the village's attention.

"Everyone! Your attention please! It is time to start our celebration! Make your way to the stands!" Zeek fanned his tail feathers once more giving them a show. The villagers perked up and started to walk towards the area taking their seats. Alcides stood by one of the fences resting his arms on it.

"Well, this feels familiar." Shakeera murmured.

Welcome everyone! Today we have a special guest with us. The one and only Shakeera the great! The one who eliminated Trents!" Zeek called out, making the village cheer and clap.

"Yep, definitely feels familiar." Shakeera stated again.

"Today we start out with our top four contenders from our village. These four will test their strength against Shakeera in a spar. A one-on-one spar until one tap out or is knocked out. The only rules are no killing." Zeek said.

"You got this Shakeera! Just remember no killing!" Alcides called out.

"Alright! I get it! No killing! Seriously, I'm not a cold-blooded killer!" Shakeera bellowed.

8

Shakeera stood in the corral waiting for her opponent to get into the ring. Her first opponent was a female that was known for her speed. The battle started out with the female running circles around Shakeera slingshot ting pebbles at her. This didn't deter Shakeera in the slightest. After observing the female's technique Shakeera collected some of the pebbles that were shot at her and took chase. After a few rounds of cat and mouse Shakeera got enough momentum to run the walls of the corral keeping pace with the female. Using the pebbles in her hand she shot them out of her nailing the female from head to toe then finally making her trip falling to the ground. Shakeera stood above her with one foot placed firmly on her back keeping her pinned to the ground.

"I give up," The female said, patting the ground in defeat.

The second opponent was a male that looked like he had more abundance of tail feathers. The feathers that flared out from the eye of his feather had a silver shimmer to them like they were made of metal. He made his move by doing the shimmy making his tail feathers fan out more making the sun reflect against his metallic feathers creating bright lights blinding Shakeera and everyone in the audience. Shakeera flinches from the bright flashes of light reflecting into her eyes. After being blinded by the male she struggled to see anything in front of her. Blue dots blinded her sight so she had to rely on her other senses for this fight. Closing her eyes she used her excellent hearing to be her eyes. After hearing the males tail feathers retract, she heard him run forward skidding half way spinning in place like a spinning top. He splayed out his tail feathers as he spun, making himself rotate his metal blades. Shakeera was uncertain of how far he was because the noise of his feathers was making as he spun.

A slight brush of wind brushed against her leg. Shakeera put up her arms to guard her body from the sting from his bladed feathers. She jumped back slightly opening her eyes trying to see what was in front of her. The blue dots had started to disappear and her vision started to return. Shakeera blinked, shaking her head clearing her vision just in time to dodge another attack from him. Once he noticed that she was able to see again, he tried to blind her again but was interrupted by Shakeera tackling him to the ground, smothering his tail feathers into the ground, coating them in dirt.

"Oh no my feathers! I give up!" The male exclaimed, holding his tail feathers in defeat.

"Alright two down one more to go. Next one!" Zeek Shakeera threw her fist into the air making the crowd cheer louder.

The next opponent was another male who looked plumper than most. He did the signature move for the males doing his little shimmy fanning out his tail feathers. He turned his attention back to Shakeera giving her a smirk gesturing for her to make the first move. Shakeera tilted her head to the side then shrugged her shoulders. She charged forward, closing the distance between them. Just as she was about to grab him, his feathers fluffed up. He rolled forward into a ball speeding away dodging Shakeera entirely. As he dodges her attack she stumbled losing her footing. Turning to lock behind her she saw that the male was flaunting his success to the crowd. Shakeera made an annoyed noise as she pivoted around then ran at him again. But he just dodged her advances again. One after another he kept dodging every attempt she made.

An idea came to her as he dodged her again. When he would dodge, he would tuck himself like a ball and roll away. She charged at him again at full force, just as expected he rolled up into a ball and dodged her speeding away. Shakeera smirked, throwing her arm behind her, making her palm face the rolling blur of feathers. A black hole opened up and a green vine shot out. She made sure not to have the thorns come out, she didn't want to kill him. When the vine shot out the crowd gasped in surprise. As the male was still spinning the vine wrapping around him keeping him in the spinning motion like a yo-yo. Shakeera yanked the vine back bringing the spinning male to her.

"Wait what the? Why can't I break free!" The male called out.

Shakeera yanked him in front of her then pulled him back making him stop then threw him underhanded making him spin in place. She pulled him back once more, rolling him in circles at her sides then launched him into the sky. Shakeera used her agile ability to her advantage. She used her surroundings to get higher and higher until she leapt up into the sky. The male finally stopped spinning for a moment. Looking around he realized he was in the air; he was about to put his arms out and fan out his tail feathers to make a safe landing when he heard a loud noise coming from below him. Looking down he saw Shakeera approaching quickly. He let out a noise of fear, as she rose up to his face with a smirk only an experienced warrior would use. She soared above him doing her own spin, landing a hard blow with her leg knocking him down to the ground creating a large dust cloud. Shakeera landed next to the male who was knocked out. There was a moment of silence before the crowd stood up and cheered loudly, they chanted her name joyfully.

"Wow..." Zeek spoke in astonishment.

"That's it everyone! Shakeera is the winner!" Zeek held up Shakeera's arm into the air as the crowd went crazy. Shakeera walked up to Alcides who was smiling big at her. She hopped over the fence dusting herself off, Alcides patted her back gently.

"Hey, good job not killing anyone this time. That must have been hard to resist the urge." Alcides chuckled.

"Yeah, yeah, yeah. I got it the first hundred times. It wasn't that bad to not kill them. Sure, it was my instinct to keep the thorns out that last battle but I kept them down." Shakeera thumbed her nose slightly.

"Good, I'm proud of you." Alcides smirked at her.

Arsena walk up to Alcides and Shakeera clapping with excitement beaming at them with excitement. Arsena came up to Shakeera grabbing her arm gently tugging her lightly. Shakeera looked at her in confusion then back at Alcides, trying to ask him what she should do.

"That was a great display of true power Shakeera. Now if you don't mind coming with me, my friends and I would love to get you ready for the dance tonight."

"A dance?" Shakeera questioned.

"Yes, a dance. After the battle the festival begins. During the festival the villagers here sell their crops and have games for the children. The dance itself is a dance of romance. To give positive energy for the years to come. Now don't you worry, you'll see your handsome mate in a few minutes. The males will take care of him." Arsena pulled Shakeera along with the other females that were giggling. The males all grinned guiding Alcides away from Shakeera reassuring him that everything will be fine.

Shakeera was led to a large building that looked like femininity was puked all over the place. Watching the females scurry around in the room picking up items and talking amongst themselves. Arsena stood in front of Shakeera smiling softly, placing her hands on her shoulder.

"Now Shakeera, if you would, remove your clothes."

"What?" Shakeera questioned defensively, her cheeks turning a light shade of pink.

"Don't worry your cute little head my friend. We're just going to get you cleaned up and get you a new outfit for tonight and mend your clothing for your travel in the morning." Arsena cupped Shakeera's face in her soft hands.

Shakeera blinked then looked away nodding her head as she took a step back slowly taking off her garments until she stood there in all her glory. She slowly started to cover herself due to her past experiences with the guards who would bathe her. The females stopped in mid action seeing Shakeera. Gasping in awe, Shakeera's skin was a nice cream color even with the dirt that was covering her body. Arsena stepped up to Shakeera followed by two other females with a warm washcloth. They started to wash the filth off of her.

"You skin is beautiful Shakeera." Arsena stated washing Shakeera's arm. Shakeera scoffed looking down at her body that was covered in scars from her past battles.

"If I didn't have all these scars, it would be better." Shakeera mumbled.

"The scars are like medals to me." Arsena said tracing an outline of one of the scars on her forearm.

"It shows that you survived what most couldn't."

"Yeah, but most guys don't find a roughed up female attractive."

"I don't believe that at all. What about your mate?"

"He's not my mate" Shakeera paused, taking a breath. "He only said that I was his wife to get free stuff from a vendor. He's just a guy that helped me escape from the hellhole that I was trapped in." Shakeera said, glancing up at the ceiling.

"I think you're making it that way Shakeera; you are very attractive." Arsena's eyes traveled up and down Shakeera's well-built body.

"So, a full-breed demon like yourself finds me- "Shakeera said while backing Arsena against the wall, hands flat against the wall on either side of Arsena's head. Arsena was about two inches shorter than Shakeera. The other females gasped in awe watching the scene unfold in front of them blushing.

"A half breed attractive? Even if I'm filth? Being half demon and half human." Shakeera finished.

Arsena gasped, her cheeks flushed. Her hands moved on their own, one going to one of Shakeera's ears. It flicked against her hand making Shakeera flinch instinctively.

"Shhh..." Arsena whispered tenderly. Her other hand wandering around Shakeera's waist finding her tail. Gently she grabbed the base of her tail connected at her waist. Shakeera made a weak gasp her body pushed up against Arsena's body. Arsena smiled as she continued to rub Shakeera's ear and tail. An unusual noise filled the room.

"Prrrrr" Shakeera's face turned pink her eyes started to get heavy.

"What a beautiful sound Shakeera. You haven't really had the chance to be feminine have you Shakeera?" Arsena asked as Shakeera buried her face against Arsena's neck, nipping it softly earning a gasp from Arsena. Shakeera pulled her head back enough to mumble out her response.

"No, since I was captured and thrown into the battle arena I was forced to act like a male since it's ran by a man and is male dominant."

"Oh, I'm sorry Shakeera that you had to go through that. Please allow us to teach you how to be more feminine." Arsena grabbed Shakeera's hand bringing her to the middle of the room.

Arsena and the females resumed cleaning Shakeera. After they finished cleaning, they took

Shakeera's measurements and proceeded to dress her. She looked at herself in the mirror at the outfit that they had put on her. She was wearing a long sleeved dark blue shirt with shimmering see through material that sparkled from the lights in the hut. They had put her in a black skirt that had a slit on the side showing off her leg.

"Well...this doesn't look too bad. I can't really walk in this thing though." Shakeera tried moving around in the skirt but it got caught on her leg a few times.

"You'll get used to it, now allow me to teach you how to be more confident with your body." Arsena came up behind Shakeera placing her hands on Shakeera's waist.

Arsena motioned for one of the females to start the music. A medium tempo song started to play. Shakeera's ears twitched to the lively music being played, she felt Arsena start moving her hips from side to side to the base beat of the music.

"Now see your hips are so curvy, it's perfect for dancing. Use your hips to follow the beat of the song just like this." Arsena demonstrated as such moving Shakeera's hips to the beat. After a few minutes Shakeera was moving on her own, Arsena slid her arms alongside Shakeera's moving her arms so they went up above her head.

"Now close your eyes and feel the rhythm and let your body do what it wants to do." Arsena took a step back observing Shakeera's dancing. At first Shakeera felt awkward dancing in front of everyone but after closing her eyes and doing just as Arsena said letting her body move with the music.

Alcides was confused why Zeek and some of the other males were escorting him in the opposite direction that Shakeera was being led. The group walked into the tent that had a variety of masculine art pieces and statues of Peaconian's. Zeek stopped in the middle of the tent posing with his hand outstretched towards Alcides.

"Alcides my friend, do you know how to dance?"

"I'm no expert but I know a thing or two." Alcides said, eyeing Zeek's hand.

"Well, Alcides I'm going to show you how to dance with Shakeeera. Knowing how she is, seeing her in action I know exactly how to control that crazy untamable stallion of a woman." Zeek called out, grabbing Alcides by the hand, spinning him into Seeks arms.

"Uh hey!" Alcides protested.

"You've seen it too, haven't you? The raw power that she harnesses. No one can control your mate but you."

"She's not really my mate alright. I just said that to get free stuff from a merchant." Alcides averted his eyes cheeks turning a slight shade of pink. Zeek made a tsk noise with his tongue shaking his head in disappointment.

"Alcides my friend, you know that's not the case here. For you and her, there is something special. I saw it happen during the battle today. You give her a special boost with her abilities. But she has been used to being by herself since she was a young girl. So, she is used to doing everything herself. So, I'm going to teach you how

93

to take the lead with someone like her." Zeek took a step back smiling down at Alcides.

"Right." Alcides said slowly. "Ok, if you want to teach me how to properly dance with Shakeera then let's get to it."

"Excellent! Now let's begin." Zeek motioned for one of the males to start the music. A lively up-tempo song started to play. Zeek held out his hand gesturing for Alcides to place his hand on his.

"Now the way to make your partner move where or how you want is as simple as a turn of your wrist." Zeek demonstrated by putting pressure on Alcides right hand making him turn out word. Zeek then pulled back gently bringing Alcides back to facing him then pulled him to face the other side.

"Now if you want to make a move like this, all you have to do is put a little pressure on the hand and just turn her the same way you're going" Zeek put pressure on Alcides hand making him turn so his arm was behind his back and they were shoulder to shoulder.

"Next, I'm going to show you a move that will show off your partner to everyone. "EEK released Alcides, taking hold of his arms making him hug himself.

Zeek used his right arm that was wrapped around Alcides waist to grab his left hand flinging him out like a rug. Zeek took a step back guiding Alcides to walk forward, showing him off like a show pony.

"Your partner is your masterpiece you have to display her to everyone like so." Zeek put on some pressure on top of Alcides hand making his step forward but keeping his hand pulled back.

As Zeek made him walk forward he put his thumb on Alcides knuckles swaying it from side to side making Alcides sway the opposite direction of his guiding hand. With a flick of his wrist Zeek whipped Alcides back to face him and did the same thing pulling Alcides towards him.

"That's the basics. I believe you will tame that wild spirit of her's." Zeek smirked. A bugle sound came from outside with what sounded like fireworks being set off.

"Sounds like it's time. Let's get you changed for the occasion." Zeek hummed as we went over to a trunk rummaging through the variety of clothes.

"Ah, here we go. Put this on." Zeek handed Alcides a navy-blue long-sleeved shirt with black pants.

"We'll see you out there." Zeek said walking with the other males outside of the hut.

After Alcides changed into his new outfit he stepped out of the hut to see the village had changed into a full bloom festival and was full of life. Lights and lanterns were hung along the huts guiding the way to all the stalls of food and games. Alcide found Zeek talking to some of the villagers at a food stand.

"There's the man of the night. Here, try this Alcides, one of our delicacies. Boar meat and vegetables from our crop with a secret sauce that has been passed down through generations."

Alcides took the container of food and took a bite. The flavors exploded in his mouth slipping down his throat making his whole body warm and fuzzy. Alcides made a very content noise as he took another bite of food.

"Mmm Shakeera would love this." Alcides commented, giving his trash to the food vendor.

"I'm sure she will. Now let's get you to your destination shall we." Zeek gestured, putting his arm out to the side.

Alcides followed Zeek admiring how lively the festival was. After a few minutes they arrived at a town square looking place where a light sounding music was being played. Villagers started to gather around waiting for the dance. Alcides stopped in the middle of the brick floor seeing all eyes were on him.

"Welcome everyone to our festival. I do hope everyone is having a blast. Thank you for waiting without any further delay let the dance begin." Zeek announced giving out a call that told the musicians to play the piece for their performance.

The music went from a soft flow to a rhythm that was fast but still slow that everyone could move to it. Alcides heard some calls coming off in the distance that brought his attention to the little parade of female Peaconian's. They were tossing out flowers as they split the line in two walking alongside the scene. Alcides eyes widened slightly as he saw Shakeera approach from behind.

By the beat of the drum Shakeera's hips followed the steady beat. Her hair was pulled back into a braid with some pieces of hair flowing over her shoulders. The top half of her outfit shimmered from the lights around her making her glow. She had her arms in front of her hands clasped by her waist. As Shakeera approached, she slowly looked upward to Alcides through her lashes smiling softly with a small blush on her cheeks. Everyone stood in awe as Shakeera made her appearance, the crowds whispered to one another about how much of a transformation from the roughed up half-bred could look so beautiful.

"Shakeera....I...uhm.... you look- "Shakeera silenced him with a finger.

"Don't...let's just get this over with before I lose all the courage I have." Shakeera whispered, holding her chin up.

"Ok." Alcides took her right hand into his left as he placed his other hand on the middle of her back.

He took the opportunity to actually look at Shakeera, not just as a fighter but as a woman. She was a normal height for a woman her age, her chest wasn't too big nor too small. Even being starved at the battle arena she wasn't skin and bones. Glancing down at their enclosed hands. She had the tiniest hands that he had ever seen. About the same size as his maid's hands were. Without even knowing what he was doing he pulled her hand up to eye level. His large hand engulfed hers. Splaying his hand out flat so their hands were pressed together.

'Such small hands...' Alcides noted mentally. But at the end of those small hands were razor sharp claws.

'Alright enough ogling' Alcides shook his head and repositioned them to their rightful position for dancing.

The beat of the song went, slow-quick quick-slow. Alcides took a step back, guiding

Shakeera to dance with him. Shakeera followed his lead like a pro. They made their rounds showing off their moves as they were taught. The two of them danced like they have been partners for years. Alcides took a step back leading Shakeera under his arm making her little sway dance showing off her body. Alcides wanted to try to do the side-to-side movement the Zeek had shown him but he was going to put a little more spin to it. He grabbed her hand making them both turn around so they were shoulder to shoulder. After swaying to the music, he placed his free hand up palm out to Shakeera who placed her hand against his. Untangling their link arms grabbing her other hand in his. He interlocked their fingers, moving their hands in rhythm as their feet. While having their hands connected, he threaded her arms through his making her hug herself pulling her close to his body. Alcides bent down slightly whispering into her cat ear that flicked in response from feeling his breath against it.

"Now when I whip you out, do a pose, I will then motion for you to come to me then we will finish this dance, with a great move."

"Ok." Shakeera sounded uncertain.

"Don't worry, it's nothing bad, trust me." Alcide straightened up.

Alcides lifted his left hand up over his head making a pose as he whipped Shakeera out making her spin in front of him. She stopped facing him with her arms elegantly above her head, her hip pushed out to the side. Her tail swayed behind her as one of her legs was posed out in front of her. Alcides smiled at her holding out his other hand beckoning her to him. Shakeera hesitated but started to gracefully run towards him jumping upright. Just as she jumped, he placed his hands on her hips lifting her into the air. Shakeera held her arms outstretched as Alcides spun them around. He slowly lowered her, pressing their bodies together. She wrapped her arms around his neck as she hooked one leg on his hip as he dipped her slightly. Alcides put her back to her regular position as the music stopped and everyone started to applaud and cheer.

"There you have it folks! Now everyone enjoy the festivities!" Zeek called out. The band started to play an up to beat music and the village was bustling with joy as everyone returned to what they were doing.

"You probably worked up an appetite, there is a food stand that you would love to eat." Alcide nodded behind him to the line of stalls that were slowly starting to get crowded.

"You had me at food. Let's go. Do you have any idea how hard it is to act girly? Let alone wearing this feminine stuff. Gahh I can't wait till I can get put my regular clothes on." Shakeera linked arms with Alcides huffing and puffing with exaggerating gestures at herself. Alcides laughed, placing his hand over hers reassuringly.

"You did fine, the best acting I've seen since you played dead for the guard."

"Hey!" Shakeera smacked him playfully. They both laughed full heartedly while they enjoyed their night at the festival.

9

Back at the battle arena a hooded female figure stayed hidden within the darkness of the forest by Zira. Amber eyes scanned the area seeing that the coast was clear. With her special eyes she was able to see clearly in the nighttime. Being light on her feet she made a dash to the opened doors staying hidden in the shadows as she snuck through the tunnel. Peeking around the corner she saw that no one was guarding the cells, she ran up to one that was opened.

"Shakeera? Hey, it's me Takeera. I'm getting you out of here?" Takeera said, walking into the unoccupied cell.

Taking off her hood her ears twitched trying to listen to all the sounds around her. Kneeling down she saw some red substance on the ground. Her heart was pounding in her chest at the fear that was her sister's blood. Dabbing her finger in it and sniffing it, it smelled like berries.

"Berries? What's going on?" Takeera questioned. Her ear flicked back hearing a noise from behind her. She whipped around seeing a group of guards trapping her in the cell.

"No!" Takeera called out as she tried to charge forward to make an escape but the guards grabbed her, subduing her. She thrashes about trying to claw and bite at them to no avail.

"Well, what do we have here?" A man's voice came from in front of her.

"You!" Takeera growled her ears flat against her head. Chase comes walking with his arms behind his back with a devilish smile on his face.

"What an unexpected surprise. Your sister just escaped from here with her new boy toy. I was all upset that she had escaped. Then her little darling twin sister, Takeera comes and basically hands herself over so we can get Shakeera back. How lucky am I?" Chase walks up to her tilting her chin up.

"What? I did not hand myself over to you!" Takeera hissed, jerking away from him. Chase chuckled.

"You remember what happened last time a certain someone came to rescue Shakeera; they barely made it out with their life." Chase said in a nonchalant tone.

"They are full-fledged demon mind you, think about it. You're a half-bred like your sister." He paused leaning in closer.

"You're probably not even as strong as your sister?" He pressed. Takeera growled low, her tail thrashing about behind her. Takeera's eyes glowed brightly as her amber eyes turned black her pupils were amber.

"How about I demonstrate how strong I really am." Takeera growled out, opening her clawed hands. Black holes appeared and black vines emerged. Little red thorns popped out from those vines. At the end of those vines were purple and red flower buds that unraveled to an exotic flower. It spun around spewing out purple poisonous spores. The guards let go of Takeera attempting to cover their faces but her spores already infected them. Takeera's vines split into multiple vines whipping around like crazy.

"Oh, interesting." Chase murmured.

Takeera's vines wrapped themselves around the guards' necks, casting them aside. Takeera's eyes locked with Chase's as she shot forward launching upwards soaring over Chase making a run for it. Takeera slid across the floor to the tunnel she came in but it was shut tight. She doubled back trying to find a way out. She ran down a hall seeing that a group of guards were in search of her. Cursing under her breath she ran in another direction accidentally smacking face first into a wall. Grabbing her face in pain, Takeera looked at the wall, seeing that one of the bricks was pushed in. The door made a humming noise. The wall split into two revealing a staircase that was leading down into a dark void. Takeera tilted her head to the side in confusion. A noise coming from behind her made her run head first into the doorway. The door closed behind her as a line of lights turned on eliminating the hallway leading down to an unknown location. Takeera walked down the spiraling stairs until she saw a green light eliminating at the bottom.

When she finally made it to the bottom of the stairs there was a large laboratory filled with large tubes filled with a green substance. The over lights blinked on, illuminating what was in those tubes. Takeera gasped, covering her mouth with what was in front of her. The tubes contained different body parts of demons connected to wires. Takeera stepped up to one of the tubes taking a better look at the demon parts recognizing them from the past battles that her sister was in.

"What is all this?" Takeera asked out loud. She jumped in surprise as a male voice came from behind her. Chase and four guards stood there with their shocking rods

"Looks like you found my other last resort plan. Once Shakeera sees that you've taken her place, no doubt she will come and save your life. Once she comes here to save the day, I will let the final form from all these strong demons destroy her, or puts her in submission whichever comes first." Chase chuckled at the end.

"You're one sick puppy aren't you." Takeera shook her head.

"You may say that. But I am a man that enjoys giving the people what they want, a show." Chase snapped his fingers and the guards advanced to Takeera, shocking her till she was unconscious. Chase walked over to a table grabbing a metallic collar and placing it around Takeera's neck.

"Now get her ready, it's time to make her great debut and get our star battler back." Chase smirked, glancing at the containers filled with demon body parts.

10

After the night's festivities came to an end Shakeera and Alcides were stumbling their way to a hut that Zeek said they could stay in for the night. After a few rounds of Zeek's special fermented berry wine, they were pretty wasted. Shakeera and Alcides were holding each other up, stumbling from one side to the other until they collided into the door frame.

"Heyyyy what's the big hm... idea pal huh? Want to start something?" Shakeera slurred at the hut's foundation.

"Now now...he didn't mean it...sorry sir...come on...let's get inside Shakeera..." Alcides dragged Shakeera into the hut, closing the door.

When Alcides turned back around he jumped in surprise seeing that Shakeera was starting to strip out of her clothes. Being as drunk as she was, she struggled to get out of her clothing.

"Ah.... come on you little bugger...oh." Shakeera was bouncing on one foot almost falling over but Alcides came to her side keeping her up.

"Hey, what are you doing?" Alcides questioned

"What? I want to get out of these things. I don't like how they feel on me." She paused and hiccupped, her face was flushed.

"I don't feel myself in these revealing things." Shakeera continued wobbling to detangle herself from the skirt.

Alcide snorted at the sight in front of him, the almighty half breed fighter struggling to change clothes. He held out his arm for her.

"Just hang on to me, ok? I don't want you to fall." Alcides offered. "I won't look ok." Alcides looked away, his face rosy from embarrassment and from drink. Shakeera made a noise and placed her hand on his arm.

"It's not like you haven't seen me naked before." Shakeera scoffed.

Alcides was about to respond when we looked back at her. She was in her bra and

110

underwear. It was a simple set of a gray sports bra and gray underwear. His face flushed red.

"You saw all my lady bits when that bastard Chase gave you the tour of the arena remember? I was getting my cleaning done after the battle." She said her blue eyes hooded, ears lopped sided.

She looked around for the clothing she was wearing, not having a care in the world that there was a male in the same room with her that could overpower her at any given moment.

"Oh, right. But still, I have more respect for you. If you're looking for your clothes they're over on the trunk."

"Oh, there you are." Shakeera giggled, padding her way to the trunk hugging her mended up clothing, then proceeded to put them on almost falling as she put her pants on. There was only one medium sized bed in the room.

"Ohhhh look at this Al! An actual bed!' Shakeera exclaimed in excitement. She ran to the bed feeling the covers on it.

"The blankest are so soft come feel it." Shakeera waved Alcides over. As he walked up to her seeing that her tail was swaying from side to side her ears were pointed forward.

'Right, she never really had a real bed before.' Alcides thought to himself.

He placed his hand on the covers feeling the soft texture. Shakeera crawled onto the bed sitting on her knees, placing her hands in front of her flat against the sheet. Carefully she started to knead the sheet in a rhythmic manner as a soft purr like noise resonated from her throat. *'Is she?'* He questioned then leaned forward to get a better understanding of what she was doing. She pulled a bit of the fabric up then pushed it down then repeated the same action with the other hand. *'Is Shakeera making biscuits? Is she purring too?'* Alcides tentatively placed his finger against her neck feeling the vibration of her purring. Shakeera then moved her head so that she was pushing against his hand.

"Uhm...are you wanting something?" Alcide asked.

"Mmm, I want scratches..." Shakeera purred out her eyes shut halfway.

112

"Where?"

"My ears dummy." Shakeera slurred out.

Alcides blinked for a moment trying to process what she was wanting. He remembered that her ears are sensitive to touch. But what better chance to get his curiosity out of the way than to do as she requested. He sat down in front of her crossing his legs. Leaning forward he placed his hands on either side of her head, his fingers barely touching her feline ears. Remembering how he would usually scratch a cat's ears he began scratching at the base of her ears. If he thought the first purr was loud, he was sorely mistaken. As he started the scratch the purr intensified louder. Shakeera pressed against his hands more.

"Just like a real cat." Alcides murmured with a smile. Shakeera peered up at Alcides, her eyes had a glossy look to them.

"You know I never asked for my life to be like this." Shakeera said, sitting with her legs crossed like Alcides.

"What do you mean?" Alcides asked.

"I never asked to be a half breed you know? I never wanted to be in the stupid battle arena either. I should have stayed with my siblings and not followed that damn blue butterfly." Shakeera's ears flicked backwards as her tail made a flop noise against the bed.

"Yeah, it was quite an event. Back when the world was 'normal'. But back then the people who were in charge thought they were doing the right thing for their people. But to only make the whole world worse. Having that nuclear war changed almost all the population into demons with only a few humans that survived." Alcide put his hands on his lap looking Shakeera over.

"Speaking about messed up things, hypothetically what if I was a prince of the West Kingdom. My parents want me to take over the kingdom and bring in an heir to the kingdom. They were trying to do an arranged marriage with the Princess of the East Kingdom."

"The East Kingdom? Her? Why?" Shakeera asked, tilting her head side.

"How would I know? They want to make an alliance with them or something like that. Don't get me wrong, she seems like a nice person but I'm not in love with her. I don't want to marry someone for politics. I want to marry someone because I love them."

"So, marrying someone is like making a pact with them? Like choosing a mate, right?"

"Yeah, that is basically what marriage is. To be bound to someone for the rest of your lifetimes. But I want to help people who are struggling in these times. Seeing how people are being treated, humans, half breeds, and demons alike. Back at Zora I saw children in the streets begging for food or money to live. No one should have to suffer while the rest sit on their ass's and waste useful resources." Alcides heard Shakeera make a sighing noise, her eyes closed slightly with a slight blush on her cheeks.

"That's what I love about you." She said softly. Alcides' heart skipped a beat.

"What?" Alcides' drunken state seemed to disappear.

"I love how compassionate you are for the little man. If what you say is true, being the prince of the West Kingdom, you can make a difference for the future of this messed up world. Makes me want to make you my mate even more now."

"Your mate?" Alcides blushed, scratching the back of his head.

"Yeah. You've treated me like an actual person and not just an object. When we were in that fight where I saved you, I felt like I had more power when I was with you. It happened again when I was fighting the warriors at the festival. But I know that you don't want to be my mate though."

"Wha what? Why wouldn't I? Did I say that?" Alcides looking around confused.

"No, you haven't said a thing, I only assumed since you know." Shakeera wrapped her arms around herself looking to the side.

"If I didn't have any ounce of affection for you, why would I break you out of that prison and take you home with me." Alcide blurted out not realizing he said it, he quickly shut his mouth

116

tight. Shakeera's eyes were wide as she blinked repetitively. Alcide cleared his throat trying to break the awkwardness between them.

"So, how does one become a mate? Like what's the process? Is there a special ritual like humans do for weddings?"

"Well, sure, you can have a 'wedding' ceremony for the family and such. But the part that makes us bound together as mates is linking our persons together."

"Ok...such as?"

"We have to mix out blood together and I leave my mark on you."

"A mark?"

"Yeah, so that others know you're mine. Don't humans have something like that?"

"Yeah, the male and female wear rings on their left hand to symbolize their bond together. They put it on the ring finger of the left hand because it is said that the ring finger is connected to the know. know. looked down at her hand holding it up trying to visualize having a ring on her hand.

"So, what do you say? Do you want to be my mate?" Shakeera asked. Alcides felt his heart beat fast. His mind is going a million miles per hour.

"Will it hurt?" Alcides asked.

"It might sting a little."

"Ok, let's do it." Alcides said. It took Shakeera a few minutes to connect the dots then it finally connected and her eyes grew big.

Shakeera sat on her knees and scooted closer to Alcides so they were eye level. She held up her index finger dragging her nail along the junction where his neck and shoulder met making a small cut. Alcides flinched slightly but watched her with curiosity in his eyes. She pricked her finger and dabbed her blood with his. Leaning forward she licked his scratch, healing it almost immediately. A small vine design appeared soon after. Shakeera was about to pull back when Alcides cupped her face in his hands.

"Would it be alright if I kissed you?" Alcides asked not taking his eyes off of her. He saw a flash of fear go across her eyes as she looked to the side.

This made him think that she hadn't had a good experience with kissing. Someone must have done something bad to her when she was in the battle arena.

"Was it the guards?" He asked, searching for the answer in her downcast eyes. Shakeera just looked up at him and nodded slowly. Then a thought came to him, his face turned serious.

"Did they...?" He pressed on, trying to get his point across. Shakeera shook her head no.

"No, they tried. That's why I was muzzled and chained up. Someone got cocky." Shakeera stated.

"Well, I'm not like them." Alcides murmured.

"I know you aren't." Shakeera whispered. After a moment of looking into each other's eyes, Alcides drew Shakeera's face closer to him. They're lips met together in a tender kiss. Shakeera stiffened for a moment on contact thinking it was going to be like how those awful guards treated her, but to find out that this kiss was more genuine and gentler. The two pulled away their cheeks flushed with a goofy smile on their face.

"I promise you Shakeera, I will be the best mate you ever have." Alcides said sincerely. Shakeera touched her lips with her fingertips then giggled.

"I have no doubt about that, now we need to get some sleep. We have a lot of traveling we need to do in the morning." Shakeera yawned big while settling down into the bed laying on her side.

Alcides returned her yawn with one of his own. As Shakeera laid down Alcides took the spot behind her with his back to the wall. Shakeera had her back to him, feeling his weight she scooted back up against him grabbing ahold of his arm pulling it so it was wrapped around her. Alcides watched as she quickly fell asleep her ears twitched every so often, He smiled while giving her one big squeeze before he too fell asleep.

11

Morning had arrived and the sun was shining beams of light through the window onto the sleeping couple. Shakeera was the first to wake up. She felt something warmth from behind her that was putting pressure on her. She groggily looked behind her seeing that Alcides's body was curled around hers, his arm was draped along her side. Her heart skipped a beat when everything finally came back to her from last night. Shakeera shifted trying to untangle herself from the sheets and Alcides. Alcides grumbled pulling Shakeera tightly against his body nuzzling the back of her head. Shakeera squeaked as she got engulfed in the big snuggle fest, her face turning pink from the closeness.

"That is the last time I drink fermented berry juice ever again." Shakeera grumbled.

"Why? You're a whole different person when you're intoxicated. Quite adorable if you ask me.'

Alcides said, opening one eye smirking at Shakeera. Shakeera blushed more as she struggled to get away.

"You and I both know that you can escape." Alcides chuckled as she glared daggers at him.

"Yeah, yeah listen here mister cuddle monster." Shakeera turned herself around poking him on the chest. She looked at the purple bruise on his neck where a little rose vine was glowing slightly. She tenderly touched the wound making Alcides twitch slightly.

"I can't believe I actually made you, my mate."

"Yeah, I couldn't believe it myself. But I'm happy you did though. It gives me a purpose in life." Alcides said while rubbing one of her ears gently. Shakeera instantly turned into a puddle of mush but shook it off scrambling out of bed panting fast.

"Alright alright! Enough! We have a lot of traveling to do now, get ready!" Shakeera called out as she started to pack their belongings.

Alcides chuckled, helping her pack as well. Alcides and Shakeera met up with Zeek and Arsena to say their goodbyes.

"Now if you two are in need of any help don't hesitate to ask for our help. You're always welcomed here in our village. We will help you in any way we can. Just give us your best call and we will come running." Zeek puffed out his chest doing a call of his own making the rest of the other villagers do their calls. Alcides did his best to mimic their calls, Shakeera just rolled her eyes and did half assed call.

"Thank you for everything Zeek. We will come and visit soon." Alcide said as he saw Shakeera start walking away.

The two started on their adventure to the west kingdom once again making great time getting to the border. Once they made it to the main road into the kingdom more people started to appear. As they passed the travelers on the road Shakeera noticed more and more people were whispering to one another. In every sentence there was one word that baffled her.

"Isn't that the prince?" One would say.

"That looks like the prince." Another would say.

Shakeera looked back at Alcides who just smiled meekly waving at them. As they came to the top of the hill the stone walls surrounded the borders of the west kingdom. On one of the walls there was a missing person flier. Alcides stopped looking at it then smacked his forehead with his hand. Shakeera walked up seeing what Alcides did then looked at the flier.

"Hey…why are there flyers with your face on it…have you seen…Prince Alcides…" Shakeera squinted then looked back and forth between the flier then back to Alcides.

"Wait… what!" Shakeera exclaimed, taking a few steps back.

"Yeah, remember that night you made me your mate? Well, remember when I said hypothetically, I was a prince of a kingdom? Well…I'm the prince of the West Kingdom." Alcide raked his fingers through his hair giving her a lopsided smile. Shakeera gawked at him. Alcides took a step forward casting out an arm gesturing for her to step in front of him.

"Welcome to my home Shakeera." Alcides stated.

Shakeera stepped forward looking at the vast bounty of the west kingdom. A large castle sits on top of a mountain overlooking the territory. She then noticed a parade of guards marching their way to her and Alcides' location. Shakeera took a step back standing in front of Alcides ears flicked back preparing to do battle. Alcides looked at her about to ask her what was wrong when he saw the guards approaching. A man on a white horse trotted up to them taking his helmet off looking down at the two.

"Prince Alcides! Thank God you're not dead. Who's this? A new servant?" The man asked.

"Hey captain Abe. No, she isn't a servant, she is my wife." Alcides wrapped his arm around Shakeera's shoulder pulling her to his side. Shakeera gasped blushing deep red.

"Sir? Your wife? But she's a half- "

"A half-bred? Yes. What about it?" Alcides interrupted.

"Ah, but what about the Princess of the east?" Captain Abe questioned.

"I didn't want to be forced to marry someone that I don't love. Now if we're done with the questions We need to get cleaned up and rest we've been through a lot and traveled a lot." Alcides said firmly, taking Shakeera's hand and started to walk to the line of guards who parted away from them.

When Alcides and Shakeera finally arrived at the castle the whole place was bustling with chaos. Shakeera heard all the comments from various people about Alcides and of her. Some worried that Shakeera would be the new maid. Where others were talking about how Shakeera was the prince's wife. While walking through the castle Shakeera looked around seeing the variety of different statues and paintings that screamed western style. Alcides walked down a large hallway stopping at a large double door that was guarded by two guards. Alcides looked around then smiled big as his personal maid came running up to them.

"Master Alcides! Thank God you're alive. Oh? Who's this?" Lili said out of breath. Alcides wrapped his arms around her hugging her tight then stepped back to Shakeera who looked Lili up and down.

"Lili, this is Shakeera, my wife. Shakeera this is my personal maid, she's been by my side since we were kids." Alcides introduced the two women to one another. Lili's head bobbed slightly as her eyes went wide, she covered her mouth gasping in shock.

"Master, I'm so happy for you! She's so beautiful." Lili beamed. "Lady Shakeera it's a pleasure to meet you." Lili bowed her head towards Shakeera.

"Oh, yes. Nice to meet you too." Shakeera mimicked.

"Alright, now with the formalities taken care of. Shakeera this is the women's bath. This is where you're going to get freshened up and uh- "As Alcides was talking Shakeera started to take her shirt off. "Wait wait wait, what are you doing?" Alcides put his hands on her shoulders stopping Shakeera from taking it off completely. Lili gasped, her face turning pink. The guards looked baffled down at her then averted their gazes from her.

"What? Aren't these guards going to hose me down?" Shakeera asked, looking at Alcides in confusion.

"No, these guys aren't going to do that. This isn't. Like where you were at before. If anything, Lili will be the one helping you bathe." Alcides nodded his head towards Lili. Shakeera looked at Alcides then to Lili.

"Someone to bathe me?" Shakeera questioned.

"Yes, now head inside, Lili will be right behind you." Alcides opened the door for her, guiding her in. Once he closed the door he turned to Lili.

"Now listen, Shakeera has gone through a lot and has been through some unfortunate circumstances due to her being a half breed and all she has known was to fight and be treated like an animal. Lili, I want you to take good care of her like you used to for me when I was a child. I've shown her the true way a man should treat her. But I want her to feel relaxed during her baths."

"What kind of circumstances?"

"She was trapped in a battle arena for a good portion of her life. After all her battles she would get hosed down like an animal. Then thrown into a cold damp cell with barely any food to eat. I want to show her that life isn't that bad."

"Don't worry Master Alcides. I will make sure she is relaxed." Lili said confidently.

Lili opened the door and quickly walked in shutting the door behind her. Glancing over she saw Shakeera standing in awe taking in her surroundings. Lili walked over to a shelf that was stocked with towels and other bathing supplies. Lili then walked up beside Shakeera placing the items on a counter. Peeking up at Shakeera she saw that Shakeera's eyes were wide with a childlike stare in wonder.

"Lady Shakeera? If you're ready, can I assist you with your bath?" Lili asked timidity. Shakeera made a noise like she was woken up from a nap. She looked at Lili for a moment then glanced at the large bathroom.

"If you would please remove your clothes." Lili held out her hand to receive them.

"Oh, right." Shakeera murmured then proceeded to remove her clothes. Lili watched in awe as Shakeera revealed her tan toned body. After stripping down to her birthday suit Shakeera handed Lili her clothing.

"Alright thank you I'll just place these here. Now if you would please stand by the shower, we can be on our way." Lili gestured towards the area where the showers were at.

Shakeera walked up to the shower area looking at the shower heads in confusion. Glancing down below the shower heads were two levers. Tentatively she reached for the right one turning it down. There was a low rumble noise traveling up from the ground to the shower head that shot out cold water making Shakeera scream and shock stumbling back away from the shower head.

"Oh God, that's cold!" Shakeera exclaimed. Lili looked over, running over to the shower turning off the cold water.

"Oh, Lady Shakeera, are you ok?" Lili inspected Shakeera over.

"Yes, I'm fine that water was just really cold." Shakeera said, wrapping her arms around herself.

"Oh, I'm sorry. Here let me get the water to the right temperature for you." Lili said while going back to the levers and proceeded to set the temperature testing the water with her hand.

"There, I think this is better. What do you think?" Lili asked. Shakeera looked between Lili then the shower. Closing her eyes and folding her ears back against her scalp she stepped into the water stream feeling the warmth enveloping her body.

"Is that better?" Lili asked.

"Yes, this is, so amazing…also better than being sprayed with cold water." Shakeera sighed in contempt. Lili smiled seeing how happy Shakeera was.

"Ok Lady Shakeera I'm going to start washing your hair, ok?" Lili stated as she went to the shelves pumping out some cream-colored liquid onto her hand then walked up to Shakeera.

"Oh, umm ok." Shakeera said. Lili pulled Shakeera back slightly, applying the liquid in her hair.

"Lady Shakeera, you have such lovely hair. It's so long and thick. How did you keep it in such good condition giving your situation I mean." Lili said, running her sudsy fingers through Shakeera's brown and blue hair making her way up to Shakeera's skull being mindful of her ears. Shakeera started to get weak in the knees as Lili started to massage Shakeera's head.

"It wasn't easy, my younger sister would bring me some dried herbs that I would put in my hair before every battle so when they sprayed me it would clean my hair." Shakeera sighed.

"Wow that is an amazing thing. Ok I'm rinsing now place your head in the water now."

Lili instructed gently guiding Shakeera's head into the water rinsing the suds out of her hair. Lili looked down at Shakeera's tail that was curled up around her hip.

"Lady Shakeera? Is there a precise way that you wash your tail?" Lili asked.

"Oh, uh not really just like how I wash my hair I guess." Shakeera looked down at her tail then back to Lili. Lili then gently grabbed her tail lathering up from the base to the tip. When Lili was at the base Shakeera made a small squeak then her tail started to twitch. Lili giggled as bubbles splashed all over her face.

"Oh, Lili I'm sorry let me- "

"No no, its fine Lady Shakeera I'm almost done." Lili washed her face off with a cloth then sprayed Shakeera's tail off. Lili stepped up to come face to face with Shakeera's. Shakeera looked down at Lili cupping the side of her face rubbing her thumb along her flushed cheek.

"Just call me Shakeera, you and I are the same. We are both half breeds. You, Miss Lili, are one of the most beautiful halves breeds I've seen in my life." Shakeera then reached behind Lili's back reaching for the zipper on her maid's outfit and started to pull it down.

"Oh…my…" Lili gasped as her outfit slumped down.

"We are more like sisters than being a servant and master base. I would like you to take a bath with me. We have the same body parts. So why are you so embarrassed?" Shakeera asked as the clothes fell to Lili's feet exposing her undergarments.

"That is true, yes. I just haven't done this since I was a child with master Alcides." Lili said bashfully. Shakeera used her skillful fingers to unclasp Lili's bra with one hand making it fall to the floor.

"Do you want me to help you with the rest?" Shakeera asked, lifting a brow.

"Oh, no no I can manage just um, go to the bath and I will join you shortly." Lili mustered as she grabbed her belongings, placing them by Shakeera's.

"Let me put your hair up, ok?" Lili went up behind Shakeera pulling her hair up into a ponytail then clipping her hair up.

Shakeera walked up to the edge of the large bath poking a toe into the warm water. After a few seconds Shakeera stepped into the bath slowly emerging herself into the warm water up to her breasts. Instantly she felt her muscles relax from her travels and years of fighting. Lili knelt down by the edge of the bath placing wash cloths and soaps down. She then stepped into the water next to Shakeera who looked like she didn't have a care in the world. Lili grabbed a sponge lathering it with soap then proceeded to wash Shakeera.

"Hey Lili...?" Shakeera asked, opening one eye.

"Yes?"

"Can you tell me about Alcides? What was he like as a kid?"

"Well, Alcides was always a caring person. He never liked politics. Whenever there was some big meeting, his parents were in and he had to be there, he would always be looking out the window at the people outside. He would finish his studies quickly then go help the people of his kingdom. No matter if the person was a human or demon or a half breed, he would always help." Lili started rubbing the sponge along Shakeera's back. Shakeera opened her eyes fully staring at the ceiling watching the steam from the bath. Shakeera leaned forward more so Lili could get more access to her back. Lili looked at Shakeera's back seeing the scattered scars from her past battles. Tracing a finger over the little white blemishes Lili sighed.

"Even with the scars your skin is beautiful, they're like tattoos that tell your story." Lili murmured.

"Yeah, I guess you're right. Now it your turn." Shakeera laughed, switching positions with Lili. Placing Lili in her lap, Shakeera started to wash Lili's back also noticing that Lili had a few scars on her pale skin.

"You know, this reminds me a lot of how my sister and I bathed when we were younger." Shakeera smiled, rinsing Lili off.

"You're quite fond of your little sister, aren't you?" Lili asked while helping Shakeera out of the bath, helping her dry off.

"Yeah. She's my twin sister. She will always be the most important person in my life." Shakeera started looking out the window seeing that the moon was shining through. Lili finished drying Shakeera off from head to toe then dried herself off as well. They both redressed themselves.

"Well Shakeera I believe dinner is ready shall we go meet up with Master Alcides?" Lili asked with a smile on her face.

"Yes, I'm so hungry right now." Shakeera chimed in. Lili opened the door for Shakeera seeing that Alcides was leaning against the wall across the hall.

"Well Shakeera? How'd you like your treatment?" Alcides asked, walking up to her.

"Well, it's a lot better than what I had before. I do have one request though. Lili here will have to accompany me whenever I bathe from here on out." Shakeera winked at Lili making her blush as she walked past her. Alcides laughed as he started to walk with Lili in tow.

"So, where is mother and father?" Alcides asked.

"They are currently in the East Kingdom talking with the King and Queen about your, uhm, disappearance." Lili said timidly.

"Oh, right that whole thing. Well, they should be happy that I have a wife now. It may not be royalty but I do love her." Alcide said with a pleased smile. He walked up to Shakeera so they could walk side by side.

"Are you ready for dinner, Shakeera? You're going to love it." Shakeera smiled big at him with a little blush on her cheeks.

"As long as you're there I know I will." Shakeera stated. The group made it to a large room that had a long table that was covered in food of all kinds. Shakeera's jaw hit the floor.

"Did I die and go to heaven?" Shakeera said in awe as a little drool seeped out of her mouth.

"In this case yes you have. Grab a plate and dig in!" Alcides exclaimed, giving her a small push.

"You don't have to tell me twice!" Shakeera boasted as she snagged a plate and started to pile on food. After seeing Shakeera sit down and scarf down her food like it was her last meal Alcides started to make his plate. Sitting down next to her he started eating. After a while one of the guards gave Alcides a remote to a large screen tv. Alcides turned on the tv and the first thing that came onto the screen was the Battle Arena. Alcides' chest grew tight when he saw who was on the screen.

"Lili get me a paper, a pen and a capsule and some rope. Hurry!" Alcides ordered.

Alcides knew what Shakeera would do when she saw this. He could feel her emotion. Lili jumped running out of the room quickly to return moments later with the items that Alcides had asked for. Writing down something quick he rolled the paper up and put it in the capsule.

"Oh! Mmmf is this a tv? What's playing...?" Shakeera looked up after stuffing her mouth full of meat but stopped mid chew as she saw who was on the screen.

"Welcome everyone to our Midnight Madness fight! I'm just as upset that our dear champion Shakeera has ran away. But don't you worry I have a special surprise for you all. Someone just as good. Give her a big applause to her sister Takeera!" Chase's voice rang from the speakers. There stood Takeera in the middle of the arena surrounded by a cluster of demons. Shakeera dropped her fork on her plate with a loud clank her blue eyes widen in rage.

"No! Takeera!" Shakeera called out pushing the chair away, knocking it to the ground. Lili jumped in fear. Shakeera's whole demeanor changed as her heart started to pound fast in her chest. Her bright blue eyes turned to a midnight blue with red pupils, blue markings appearing on her cheeks. Her long brown hair whipped wildly behind her; her hands started to shake as her nails grew like daggers. Both of her palms had black holes that appeared revealing her rose vines with red thorns whipping around like crazy. A low growl came from her mouth as she darted out the door. Right before she could leave Alcides had tied a rope around her waist hanging on for dear life.

"Chase is a dead man!" Shakeera roared.

12

Shakeera launched herself and Alcides out of the castle doors sprinting to the stone walls that surrounded the castle. Alcides held on to the rope that he had tied around Shakeera's waist apologizing for the chaos Shakeera was creating. Shakeera then skidded to a halt for a moment as the towers were a few yards away. Alcides pulled himself up trying to look in Shakeera's eyes to see if he could talk some sense into her.

"Hey Shakeera are you alright? What are you going to do?" Alcides asked. Shakeera jerked her head in his direction as if she heard him from a distance.

"Alcides .... if you're not going to help me then stop holding me back. I have to save Takeera. I will not allow her to endure what I had to deal with just because I ran away." Shakeera growled out.

"I'm going to help you, that's what mate's do right? I don't want anything to happen to your sister either. We just need some help. On our way there try your best to go by the Peacockians village. I think they might be able to help us. I'm going to give them this letter so they can meet us there." Alcides waved the container in front of her face.

"Hold on tight then." Was all Shakeera said as she launched out two vines latching on to two pillars pulling them tight. It took Alcides a few seconds to understand. He wrapped his arms around her shoulder and her side right before she whipped her vines, rocketing them into the air. Alcides looked over his shoulder seeing his home becoming smaller and smaller by every bound Shakeera took. The full moon illuminated their surroundings just as the sun did. Alcides noticed they were going through the forest where their new friends lived. When Shakeera leaped high into the sky Alcides took the opportunity to look around until he saw the familiar glow of the village.

"Ok Shakeera, can you try to fly over the village so I can give them my message?" Alcides called out. Shakeera grunted changing her direction of her descent. Just as they were approaching the village Shakeera jumped from tree to tree until she found a large tree to use to pull them higher and faster so they would rocket overhead. Alcides tried his best to make the call of the Peacockians several times. When they got over top, he let out the loudest call he could make. He heard their calls seeing Zeek in the middle of the crowd. He chucked the vessel down to Zeek who caught it.

"No time to explain! Just read my letter! Hurry!" Alcides called out just as they left out of sight of the village.

Takeera opened her eyes slowly, seeing that she was in Shakeera's cell shackled up just as her sister was. Pushing herself up she sat against the wall using her cat ears to hear around her. All she could hear was machinery noises with a low rumble of footsteps and the echo of groups of people. Takeera hit the ground with a loud clank noise as she tried to wiggle her way out of the shackles to no avail.

"Tsk." Takeera scoffed in annoyance.

"Great job Takeera, see what you got yourself into now?" Takeera grunted trying to pull at her chains again.

"Now you have to fight for your life just because you wanted to save your twin sister." Takeera said, rolling her neck slightly, popping it in the process. A door opened and closed making Takeera stand her guard. Her ears went flat against her skull as she bared her fangs at the guards who walked up to the cell.

"Come now girly it's your time to shine." One guard said as he opened the door letting the other guards in with their shocking sticks. Takeera growled low as she struggled to stand. With the guards surrounding her they escorted her to the waiting area of the opponents. The guards quickly unshackled Takeera, almost losing a few fingers in the process. Right when she was released from her bounds she spun around chasing after them just to get the gate slammed in her face. Takeera cursed under her breath walking back to her spot. The overwhelming noise of her surroundings was almost deafening, from the noise of the loud speakers to the noises of the audience above her.

"For ten long years, this is what Shakeera had to do every single day." Takeera commented as the loud speaker clicked on a booming voice resonated from them. Once the voice came, Takeera instantly hissed in disgust.

"Welcome everyone to our Midnight Madness fight! I'm just as upset that our dear Champion Shakeera has run away. But don't you worry I have a special surprise for you all. Someone just as good. Give her a big applause to her sister Takeera!" Chase's voice rang, making the crowd roar in excitement.

The gate opened and the spotlights were put on her as Chase called out Takeera's name. The audience were in awe trying to get a good look at Takeera as she walked out onto the battlefield. Takeera stopped in the middle of the arena taking in her surroundings. The stands were full of bodies young and old, all eyes were on Takeera. She stood there with the lights casting upon her figure. Her dark brown hair waved behind her; the dark blue highlights seemed to glow under the light. Takeera's chipped ears moved every which way to the sounds around her. Takeera wasn't as built as Shakeera but she did have some muscle on her. Her dark brown tail that had blue fur on it swayed behind her in excitement. The tip of her tail had a notch on it so it was bent at an angle.

"Let's get this show on the road! Bring out our contenders!" Chase's voice called out as a siren went off. The gates surrounding Takeera opened simultaneously releasing the demons. Takeera smirked, flicking out her wrists let her dark vine's slither out whipping around with excitement.

"Alright sis, I'm going to make you proud. Bring it on!" Takeera called out, initiating the battle.

Hours passed and Takeera beat every contender left and right. Takeera stood there covered in her opponent's blood, out of breath she held her fist in the air making the audience cheer. Chase stood in his office that overlooked the arena biting his thumb in irritation. The cleanup crew started to take the dead bodies out of the arena for the halftime break.

"How is she that good? She's almost as good as Shakeera but she never had the experience in the arena." He looked up, seeing over the walls of the arena barely being able to see the lights of Zira. He could see that the sky started to get lighter, the sun was slowly coming over the horizon.

"Doesn't matter I put my message out there, wherever Shakeera is it's only a matter of time until she comes to save the day." Chase chuckled, grabbing his microphone and clearing his throat.

"Alright everyone, how's everyone enjoying the show so far?" Chase called out. The audience responded with a loud cheer. Takeera heard his voice turning her attention up at the windowed office that towered over the arena. Her ears flicked back as she whipped her vines, flicking the blood that coated them off.

"Hey! The all-mighty Chase sitting in your comfortable castle. I have beaten all your damn pets. What else do you have for me huh? Why don't you come down here and fight me instead!" Takeera called out. Chase chuckled, stepping closer to the window looking down at Takeera with pure amusement on his face.

"Don't you worry my dear Takeera, I still have a few more surprises for you. Now for our next contender, Big red!" Chase announced. A horn went off as the gate opened up to a pitch-black room. Takeera looked at the gate only seeing pitch blackness, when a cluster of beady red eyes appeared. Ruby red needle-like legs appeared walking forward revealing a large female arachnid came into the light. From her head to her waist line was human but from the waist down was the body of a spider.

"A special surprise for our fans today, a female fighter. "Chase called out.

"Mmmm a little kitty, looks like a snack to me." Big red chuckled right before she rushed forward charging at Takeera.

Takeera nearly dodged Big Red's attack. Running on all fours Takeera put distance between them skidding to a halt. Before she knew it big red was on her again with so much force pinning her down with her needle-like legs. Takeera was barely able to hold her back. Her ears flat against her skull she hissed baring her fangs.

"Oh, you're a fast one." Takeera struggled.

"From what I hear half breeds taste like under ripe potatoes." Big red stated, leaning more against Takeera making a disgusted expression.

"Sorry to disappoint you." Takeera pushed back her arms, shaking from the weight of big red.

"Oh, I'm not worried, I can tolerate it once I inject my venom in you, dissolving your innards then you will taste a lot better" Big red smiled big revealing her large fangs that dripped with her poisonous venom. The liquid dripped beside Takeera's head burning the ground.

"Yeah, I'd rather not. I want my insides to be in one piece, thanks." Takeera pulled her legs up to her chest pushing up from the ground landing a kick to Big red's chin making her stumble backwards from the sudden burst from Takeera. As Big red stumbled back Takeera took the opportunity to shoot out her vines wrapping them around Big red's neck landing on her back.

"Whoa their girl whoa!" Takeera laughed as Big red scrambled to get her bearings.

"Oh, we're playing it this way huh? Are you going to fight me or what?" Takeera taunted.

Big red reared up and started rampaging around the arena slamming her body against the walls. With a flick of her wrist her vines grew thorns that dug into Big red's skin making her scream in pain. Big red reached around and yanked Takeera off of her, tossing her in the air. Takeera was launched in the air passing the walls and she adjusted herself seeing something from the corner of her eye. She looked over to see a speck jumping in the air. Squinting her eyes she finally made out the speck.

"Shakeera?" Takeera gasped as she started to fall back to the ground. Takeera rotated so she would go head first to see Big red waiting for her with open arms, better yet open mouth. Big red opened her mouth wide, shooting a web like substance from her mouth coating Takeera from head to toe. Takeera crashed to the ground unable to move with the wet substance binding her limbs to her body. Fighting against her restraint she wiggled and thrashed about trying to get free but to no avail. Looking up she saw Big red stalking her way to Takeera.

"Games over little kitty time to die." Big red chuckled looming over Takeera venom dripping from her fangs.

Shakeera and Alcides were getting closer to Zira. She saw the light beams shining in the sky, knowing that Takeera was fighting for her life. When Shakeera launched herself in the air, she saw a small dot rising over the walls of the battle arena she knew it was Takeera. Shakeera growled low as she landed at the gates of Zira making a mad dash to the battle arena. Alcides noticed that they were approaching the arena at an alarming speed.

"Shakeera drop me off here!" Alcides called out almost being ejected off of Shakeera as she skidded to a stop. The whiplash from the ride almost made him fall to the ground as his legs were jelly.

"I'm going to try to find Chase, you get your sister."

"Alright, and hey." Shakeera walked up to Alcides that was about to run. "If you really think this mate power thing is real then I'm going to need to use some more of your power."

"Wha-?" Alcides was cut off when Shakeera grabbed the front of his shirt, yanking him down to her level pressing their lips together. A surge of energy surged between the two of them giving them a second wind of energy. Shakeera pulled back looking him in the eye.

"Don't die alright. It shouldn't take long to save my sister." Shakeera said confidently.

"I won't?" Alcides said, still feeling awestruck from their kiss.

Shakeera giggled, patting his cheek affectionately while running a distance from the battle arena. She seemed to have returned back to her normal half-bred self. The look in her eyes said different as they were full of rage and determination. Making long strides she leapt into the air clearing the walls of the battle arena letting out a mighty roar she soared into the arena.

13

Takeera fought against her resistances as Big red stepped up to her towering above her. Fangs chattering together salivating over her next meal when all of a sudden, a loud roar boomed overhead causing her and Takeera to look up. The audience covered their ears from the loud sound turning their attention upwards. There was Shakeera soaring over the walls letting out a mighty roar.

"What the hel- "Big red squinted her eyes but got cut off as a thorn vine shot down her throat. Shakeera slammed to the ground standing proud as the audience cheered loudly. "What the hell are you?" Big red tried to talk.

"Tsk tsk tsk" Shakeera clicked her tongue. "Didn't your mother ever tell you it's impolite to talk with your mouth full?" Shakeera stated with a smirk as she whipped her vine that was still lodged in Big red's throat. Whipping her vine over her head she flung Big red around the stadium a few times then yanked on the vine decapitating big red mid snap. Shakeera recalled her vine running up to Takeera helping her out of the webbing.

"Shakeera, what are you doing here?" Takeera asked, standing upright.

"Here to save your ass that's what. Now let's- "

"Welcome home Shakeera. Our favorite champion has finally returned." Chase's voice echoed out of the sound system. Shakeera peered up at Chase hissing at him.

"Yeah, I'm so happy to be back at the place that kept me captive for ten years! Now I'm here to stop you." Shakeera called out about to jump when Chase made a tsk noise moving his finger from side to side.

"Now, now. You don't want to be doing that now do we?" Chase taunted. Pushing a button making a large screen turn on that overlooked the field. It was an overview of a forest area that had a large man-made home with a little farm next to it. The screen zoomed in revealing four figures. A human male with shaggy brown gray hair that looked to be in his forties. A younger male with brown hair and elf like ears and a woman with short bobbed brown hair with cat ears. They were all working in the field as a large cat creature walks up to them with a large basket in its mouth. The older male got up from his knelt position and walked up to the cat creature giving it an affectionate kiss on its head.

"Mom!" Both Takeera and Shakeera exclaimed.

"Now if you do anything out of line a bomb filled with poison gas will be dropped, killing your whole family. You don't want that now do you?" Chase taunted. Shakeera clenched her jaw growling low.

"If you do as I say nothing will happen to them got it?" Both Shakeera and Takeera nodded their heads. "Now, how about we have fight between sisters eh? A battle to see who is the stronger sibling." The crowd was conflicted but cheered nonetheless. Shakeera sighed cracking her neck walking to the middle of the arena motioning Takeera over. Takeera walked up to her.

"Well let's give them a show, shall we?" Shakeera murmured.

"But sis I don't want to fight you." Takeera protested. Shakeera bared her fangs at Takeera but swished her tail from side to side in a motion that only her and Takeera knew as communication. It was a sort of morse code.

'I have a plan, it's just like how we used to play when we were kids, play fight' Shakeera shook her tail.

'Oh, ok that's fine' Takeera swished her tail back hissing at Shakeera.

'I will be saying some mean stuff, don't take it to heart just play along' Shakeera ears flicked back as she held her head high.

"How about it lil sis? Fight me. See if you can actually be better than me." Shakeera called out as they circled each other.

"Hah you're funny didn't you see me out here? I held my own. Oh, right you didn't because you ran like the coward that you are." Takeera spat. The crowd gasped.

"Oh, the pipsqueaks that you battled were small fry to who I battled. All you ever battled were the weak creatures in the forest. If I hadn't come and saved your ass when I did you would have been a husk of a being. I battled worst enemy's my first year being here when I was eight."

"Yeah? We'll all of this could have been avoided if you hadn't run after that stupid butterfly during our hunting lessons! Mom wouldn't have been severely injured trying to get you back either!" Takeera screamed. Shakeera stopped dead in her tracks.

"Ohhhh" The audience gasped.

Shakeera's demeanor changed in an instant. Takeera's eyes grew wide and her ears drooped slightly. She knew she crossed the line that time. Takeera unknowingly let her personal feelings come out instead of the fight play taunting. Takeera could feel the sheer power radiating off of Shakeera. She wasn't top champion for ten years straight for nothing.

159

"Shakeera, I- "Takeera stammered. Shakeera held her arms out to her side, her head tilted to the side with a sly smirk. Her palms positioned splayed outward; her vines slithered out whipping about madly.

"Really little sister, it's been way too long. With my ten-year absence, why don't you show me what you've learned." Shakeera charged at Takeera slamming into her with thunderous power. Takeera was barely able to throw her vines up to counter the attack.

Chase watched the fight unfold from his office. Stepping to the side he went to a large table pouring himself a drink. He sat down on his large sofa getting the perfect view of the fight going on below him. A knock at his door brought him back to reality.

"Come in." Chase called out.

The door opened then clicked shut as footsteps were heard approaching the couch some weight pressed against Chase's back as if someone was resting their hands on it. Slowly taking his attention away from the fight he glanced up behind him seeing Alcides peering down at him.

"Oh, hello there Alcides. Long time no see." Chase spoke sheepishly.

"Yes, it has been some time since we last talked. When you threw me in a cell to fend for myself with the top man killing champion." Alcides started walking around the couch taking a seat next to Chase. Alcides looked out the window to see Takeera and Shakeera fighting, the crowd was just eating it up. Alcides returned his attention back to Chase who had a confident smile like it was just a normal thing to sit and watch a show.

"Well, yes, I did do that but I knew you could handle yourself. You are a strong man Alcides. You are a very smart man as well, tricking my guards like you did and stealing Shakeera from me." Chase looked down at his cup swirling the contents around.

"Yes, but here's the thing Chase." Alcides crossed his leg over his knee, his arms resting behind him. "You took an innocent eight-year-old girl from her family. Just to entertain people, just to take their hard-earned money just to see her die." Alcides' voice grew more annoyed.

"Now Alcides, don't make me out to be the bad guy here. You and I both know I didn't create the fundamentals of human, demon, half breed laws." Chase pointed a finger to the window.

"Yeah, but you abused the system. How many lives were taken because of your messed up entertainment." Alcides stated looking at Chase from the corner of his eye. The room was quiet except for the muffled sound of the cheers from the audience. Alcides leaned forward resting his elbows on his knees, his chin resting on his hands.

"You also broke a law doing all this too." Alcides added.

"What law?" Chase laughed looking at Alcides.

"You endangered the prince of the west kingdom and his wife."

"The prince?" Chase's brows furrowed looking Alcides up and down. Alcide stood up looking down at Chase arms behind his back eyes glowing slightly from the overhead lights.

"My name is Alcides Rockstins. The hare of the west kingdom. The woman down there fighting her sister is my wife." Alcides announced. Chase's eyes widened and the color drained from his face. He cleared his throat, loosening his shirt collar giving his best poker face.

"What do you plan on doing then?" Chase asked. Alcides smirked, cracking his knuckles.

"I'm going to put you in your place and defend my wife's honor!" Alcides grabbed Chase by his shirt lifting him up in the air then threw him over the couch and onto his desk breaking it on impact. Chase struggled to stand up. He stood on wobbling legs trying to fix his messed-up hair.

"Alcides, let me explain. I didn't know it was you at the time, a simple mistake." Alcides walked up to him grabbing him once more by the back of his head smashing his face against the glass window making a crack appear.

"Yeah, and how many unexpected people had to die because of what you did." Alcides let Chase go stepping back.

"Now since you think you've done nothing wrong; I will let you plead your case and fight back. Convince me that you're not a bad guy that I should kill right now." Alcides watched as Chase struggled to gather his composure panting with frustration.

Shakeera had Takeera pinned down on her back pushing her forearm against Takeera's chin when she heard the lightest 'ting' noise from above. Glancing up she saw that Alcides had Chase pressed against the window. Knowing that was the single to get ready. Her attention returned back down at her struggling twin sister. Shakeera growled at Takeera getting her attention. Shakeera's tail flailed about once more indicating she had another message.

It's almost time now, push me back, I will fall, wrap your vines around me throw me into the air

Ok

164

Shakeera leaned back slightly as if adjusting her position and Takeera kicked her off sending her skidding away losing balance falling onto her back. Takeera rushed forward jumping over Shakeera wrapping her vines around Shakeera swinging her around then sent her soaring into the air.

Alcides stood there waiting for Chase to fight back. He could see that Chase was losing his composure by the second. Chase kept raking his fingers through his hair attempting to fix it but making it worse by ever swipe. His face was contorted as all the emotions flashed across his face.

"How would you know anything about our world? Huh?" Chase seethed.

"You entitled little brat born with a silver spoon in your mouth. You would never understand the struggles of us the poor. You had everything given to you no question asked." Chase said trying to land a punch on Alcides but Alcides would dodge the punch without putting much effort.

"Sure, I was fortunate to be born in an upper-class family but didn't always use my higher-class status to run my life. Instead, I helped the people in my kingdom. I never held my head high and became pompous."

"Pompous? You don't even know the meaning of " pompous." Chase grabbed his glass chucking at Alcides who moved to the side making it crash against the window.

"Clearly, you're not a true man. You hide up in your tower watching the pawns of your game fight. You treat them like animals when they are living beings with life's they want to live. Come show me your true power, give me all you got." Alcides stood by the window. Chase let out a war cry charging at Alcides making them both collide into the window shattering it into pieces as the both of them fell through it.

Shakeera saw the window break just as she was flung into the air in the same direction as Alcides and Chase. She launched her vine out wrapping around Alcides and yanked him to Takeera who caught him before he could hit the ground. Using the trajectory from the force of pulling Alcides she launched herself to Chase. Chase barely had time to register what was going on as he looked in front of him seeing Shakeera rocketing at him. Shakeera punched him in the gut, shooting him in the air. She jumped to the shattered window and launched herself in the air following Chase into the sky rising higher than him. Chase watched Shakeera as she rose above him looking down at him with so much hatred in her eyes.

"Shakeera...wait. I." Chase struggled to speak. Shakeera just growled flipping forward slamming a powerful kick on his head sending him spiraling down to his tower. Shakeera landed on the ground like she was floating. The audience roared with excitement, Takeera and Alcides came to Shakeera's side.

"Good job Shakeera you did it!" Alcides exclaimed, wrapping his arms around her, lifting her up and spinning her around.

"That was awesome Shakeera, you sure gave him the business." Takeera fist pumped the air.

Shakeera laughed as she was spun around but something didn't feel right. There was an uneasiness in the air, like the calming before the storm. Alcides put Shakeera down knowing something was wrong. He could feel her body was going rigid. Shakeera looked at the once ominous tower that Chase had always loomed over watching her. Smoke started to appear from the hole Shakeera had created. A loud boom shook the stadium, making the audience scream in fear looking around trying to see what the commotion was about. Takeera looked up at the smoke that was growing more and more monstrous by the second. The gray plume of smoke grew darker with green and blue lights intermittently shining through. Takeera then realized what was happening.

"Shakeera, we need to leave now!" Takeera panicked.

"Takeera what's going on?" Shakeera briefly looked at Takeera, seeing the fear in her eyes.

"Chase had a plan 'B' if you hadn't come back and I didn't make it through his test. He has a secret lab that he kept all the best competitors you had difficulty fighting in containment tubes. He had their body parts conserved to make a fiercer champion. From the looks of that smoke, you landed him smack dab in the middle of that lab." Takeera pointed out. The ground shook again making the audience cry out in fear again. A loud booming voice shook everyone's cores.

"SSSSHHHHAAAAAAKKKKKEEEEERRRAAA AA!" It bellowed. The tower shook as a large appendage appeared grabbing onto the edge of the tower making it crumble under its sure weight. Another arm of a different color appeared beside it straining to pull out of the rubble. Once it had a grip on the side of the building it pulled itself out revealing a grotesque mismatched monster. It looked like something from a Frankenstein novel. The tower collapsed from the sheer weight of the monster sending it sliding onto the ground shaking the area around it.

"That's Chase?" Shakeera exclaimed.

"Yes, it is." Takeera said in disgust.

Chase looked at his surroundings, blinking his multiple sets of eyes when he finally saw his prize below him. He stomped his feet as he slowly approached the group below him. He then glanced up at the monitor that had him plastered in full screen. He did a double take looking down at himself holding up his mutated hands. His body jiggled around as he inspected himself then he looked back down at Shakeera.

"Look what you did to me!" Chase bellowed, smashing the screen with his fist. "You turned me into a monster!"

"In all fairness you turned yourself into this." Shakeera snickered. "If you had not created that lab full of those monster parts and kept them alive you wouldn't have been turned into this disgusting creature. But in all fairness, it suits you quite well if you asked me. It matches how you are inside!" Shakeera called out.

"Why you little!" Chase brought his arm back aiming to punch the ground in front of the group. Shakeera and Takeera jumped up dodging the impact, grabbing Alcides in the process, placing him with the crowd.

"You stay here ok." Shakeera said, kissing the top of his head. "Good job getting him down here. Alright Takeera you ready for the fight of your life?" Shakeera clenched her fists.

"Yeah, let's give him what he deserves." Takeera called out.

Shakeera and Takeera leapt from the stands starting to do their attacks on Chase. Shakeera made a large thorny sword in her hand and proceeded to attack Chase's legs as Takeera created purple bombs from her vines, throwing them at him. Chase took in a breath extending his large belly then opened his mouth as a green smog erupted out of his mouth covering the arena so there was no visibility whatsoever. Takeera and Shakeera stood on the field unable to see and could hardly breathe.

"Hey! Takeera, can you create those rotating flowers? Use them to clear the field?" Shakeera called out.

"Yeah, hold on a second." Takeera called back. Takeera's vines slithered out with little pods on them. She whipped her vine scattering the pods into the air surrounding the battle field. The pods opened up revealing flowers with three stems above them that were intertwined making them spin around quickly clearing the smog from the area. Just as the last bit of smog was dispersed Chase swung his arms out smacking Shakeera and Takeera into the walls. They groaned while pulling themselves out of their holes falling to their feet.

"I kinda got used to not being hit that hard when I left this place." Shakeera groaned, pressing on her back.

"Yeah, I'd rather not have that happen again. Let's finish this guy off now, ok?" Takeera twisted her side slightly, earning a loud crack.

"Yeah, let's finish this." Shakeera held out her hand making a large vine that looked like a large sword with spikes coming from the blade. Takeera made sei (Ninja daggers) out of her vines. Both girls charged forward unleashing attacks against Chase.

Alcides watched from the sidelines with the rest of the audience. He felt like he had to do something but there wasn't much he could do with how Chase is now. Shakeera and Takeera kept up with their attacks but kept getting knocked away. Alcides glanced up, noticing that the sun was starting to rise. He then heard the familiar sounds of the Peacockians off in the distance.

"Yes! They can help us now." Alcides got up from his seat but the noise from the crowd brought his attention back to the fight. Chase had both Shakeera and Takeera in his grasp, tightening his hands around them making them scream out in pain.

"No Shakeera!" Alcides called out. He had to think fast, then an idea came together. He remembered when he first got captured that the crowd was chanting for Shakeera. If he could get the audience to work together with him, they could help the girls out. Standing up on his seat Alcides waved his arms around calling out to the audience.

"Listen everyone, if you don't want Shakeera to die by the hands of this monster you must help them. You need to make this noise to help them out." Alcides made the peacock noise. At first the crowd couldn't hear him but after a few minutes the crowd mimicked him. Shakeera gritted her teeth as the vise grip grew tighter pushing out all her breath. She winced looking back at Alcides who had the audience doing the peacock call. Chase looked around seeing this and roared out loudly trying to silence them but that only encouraged them more. As the sun rose the shadow from the walls started to lower. The audience from the opposite side all pointed over the wall drawing everyone's attention to the now louder sounds of peacock calls as a large group of people rose over the walls harmonizing with everyone's call. Alcides craned his neck smiling big seeing Zeek and his whole village had showed up.

"Hello my friends, we are here to assist you!" Zeek called out doing his shimmy fanning out his tail feathers. The audience cheered loudly seeing the army of Peacocks beings standing on the walls ready to battle.

"Alright! Zeek! Let him have it!" Alcides called out.

14

Alcides called out Zeek's name which got the attention of all the other people around him. They started to chant Zeek's name encouraging him to fight. It was music to his ears, puffing out his chest he made another call to get his villagers attention.

"Come now everyone! Battle formation now! Give them everything we got!" Zeek called.

They all responded to him in full agreement. The males all took flight with the females strapped to them. As they lifted themselves into the sky creating a curtain along the one side of the battle arena. The males fanned out their tails catching the sun rays on their tails causing a blinding light that reflected into Chase's eyes blinding him making him drop Shakeera and Takeera to the ground to shield his eyes. Shakeera cheered big seeing Zeek and everyone from the village. As Chase called out in pain Zeek did another call out for the females to do their attack. The females pulled out their pipes readying to fire. All at once they took their shot, shooting their poison darts at Chase coating him with their darts. Chase roared in anger trying to brush off the darts as the poison started to take over his senses. Chase swung his spiked tail around shooting out the spikes towards Zeek, but Zeek came prepared. Zeek ordered them to put up their shields. Right when the spikes hit their shields the ricochet off and got sent back to Chase who wasn't expecting the attack.

"No! This can't be happening!" Chase screamed rampaging about.

"I am superior in every aspect! I am a demon! I am stronger than anyone!"

"You forget something all mighty one!" Shakeera called out sarcastically.

"What?" Chase called out looking downward to Shakeera

"It doesn't matter the size you are but how you use your strength that matters." Shakeera called out.

Shakeera runs at him dodging all his attacks that he throws at her. Takeera followed Shakeera's example and mimicked her attacks but on the opposite side. This went on for about thirty minutes.

"You got this Shakeera!" Alcides cheered.

"You half breed scum have no right to have happiness, you all were mistakes to begin with." Chase chastised.

"Oh, and who gave you the right to be the one to dictate what we can and cannot enjoy in life?" Takeera landed a thorned vine slap to the face.

The Shakeera kicked him in the back of his head using it as a jump off point. She lifted herself into the air looking down at Chase. She held out a hand to Takeera.

"Come Takeera, let's end his wretched existence for good!" Shakeera shot out her vine towards Takeera who did the same, intertwining her vines with Shakeera's. Shakeera pulled Takeera to her clasping their hands together. She pulled her sister close to her whispering.

"Now we are going to combine our vines and the biggest thorns we can make with the most poison we can produce. We're going to cut that monster into bits." Shakeera instructed.

Their vines bulked up creating a circular saw shape the thorns grew ten times their original size. Shakeera and Takeera curled against each other then started to spin in the air launched forwards charging a full-frontal assault. Chase attempted to swipe them away but got his arm sliced clean off. The grotesque appendage fell to the ground twitching and flopped around. Within seconds the arm started to dissolve in a lump of goo. The spiked ball thrashed the ground breaking up the dirt with their spikes.

"Who do you think you are! Huh? I am perfection! I am the definition of power! Your filthy half breeds can't beat me!" Chase swung his arm at another attempt of an attack. The ball rolled up the wall then pushed off, slicing off Chase's other arm. Chase screamed in pain stomping the ground around him.

"No! No! No!" Chase called out his eyes wide with rage. Chase in his disoriented mind he looked around in search of Shakeera. After finding her he opened his mouth wide shooting out a stream of fire at Shakeera and Takeera setting them ablaze. The audience gasped in fear seeing the now fireball rolling about setting the area around it on fire.

"Shakeera!" Alcides called out!

As Shakeera and Takeera were rolling around the flames did nothing to them but aid them in their fight. Shakeera nudged Takeera to get her attention then nodded. Still spinning the large spiked fireball split into two smaller spiked fireballs. Shakeera and Takeera circled around Chase, trapping him in a ring of fire. Chase tried fighting back by swinging his spiked tail but that got cut off in the process. Takeera collided to the back of his legs cutting his achilleas heel making him fall to his knees. He went down shaking the stadium. Shakeera stood in front of him as Takeera stopped on the other side of him.

"You keep going on about half breeds being nothing in the world. We have more in us than you think. Because of the hardships that you put us through, put an extra layer of wall around our hearts. That wall keeps us from letting the pain that you inflicted upon us drive us down to the darkness. Look at you now. Look what two measly 'weak' half breeds that have brought you down to your knees." Shakeera boasted.

Chase growled opening his mouth to shoot out another attack when suddenly Shakeera shot out her rose vine grabbing a hold of his tongue. Chase thrashed about trying to talk buy with a flick of her wrist her thorns popped out puncturing his tongue.

"Didn't your mother ever tell you not to talk with your mouth full?" Shakeera asked, shaking her head. Chase started to panic trying to chomp on her vines. With a sudden jerk of her wrist Shakeera ripped Chase's tongue out making an "Oops" motion with her mouth.

"Whoops cat got your tongue huh?" Shakeera laughed hysterically.

Chase screamed as blood flooded out of his mouth. Her eyes grew dark with hatred as she casted his tongue to the side. She held her palm out to Chase, her vine shaking vigorously then shot out like a gun right into his chest. The vine wrapped itself around his heart constricting it slowly. Chase gasped in surprise as he could feel the pressure on his heart grow more and more painful. He started to struggle to breath, he looked into Shakeera's eyes.

"Alright enough with my games. Now in front of everyone here. Today is the day that I Shakeera, A filthy half breed. Finally gets to beat the tyrannical all mighty Chase. Do you have any last words?" Shakeera asked.

Chase coughed up more blood looking down at Shakeera then looked at the crowds in the stands that just sat there cheering for Shakeera. He looked down at Shakeera again. He struggled to get the words out due to his tongue being torn out.

"Vile vermin." Chase gushed out one last time until Shakeera yanked her arm back, yanking out his heart from his chest.

She squeezed out all of its contents, dropping it to the ground as Chase fell face down onto the ground. Shakeera walked up to the body of Chase seeing that his body started to dissolve into goop revealing the human body underneath. She walked up the human body putting her foot on top of it, punching the air causing a massive uproar from the audience. All of a sudden Shakeera was swooped up into the air being spun around by Alcides. Shakeera laughed as she was placed on his shoulder being paraded around. Zeek called out from above flying down from above.

"There you all have it! Shakeera is the winner of this fight! Tonight, we feast!" Zeek flared his feathers out as his villagers flew down as well doing their victorious calls. Alcides placed Shakeera down feeling like a big boulder of relief has been taken away.

"So, Shakeera? What are you going to do now with the battle arena?"

"Well, there's still going to be fights." Shakeera scratched the back of her head.

"What? After everything you went through?" Alcides exclaimed.

"Now, hear me out. Ok. There are going to be a lot of changes here. Like for one. New employment will be done. Getting rid of all the bad guards here is the first thing that's going to happen. Next The homeless half breeds will be working here. The battle arena is a place where anyone young or old, human, half breed, or demon can come to enjoy a show. But there will be no fight to the death. It will be until you are unable to battle. We will have medics here to heal them. We will also have classes to teach others how to defend themselves." Shakeera declared. Looking back at Takeera that stood a little way smiling at her.

"But there is something I need to do first. Will you come with me? We will be back for the feast." Shakeera held out her hand to Alcides. He looked at her, seeing the nervousness in her eyes. He grabbed her hand rubbing his thumb over her knuckles.

"I will follow you to the ends of the world." Alcides looked deep into her eyes.

Shakeera and Alcides followed Takeera into the woods as of Shakeera's request. They walked for about two hours to the point where the forest had thickened up with trees. Flashes of images seemed to appear around Shakeera as her surroundings seems to look more familiar. Even the smells seemed to bring her back to when she was a kid before the kidnapping.

"We're almost there just a little more, oh look its- "Takeera was interrupted as someone dashed through the trees tackling Shakeera full force hugging her tightly. Shakeera was about to fight back when a familiar scent tickled her nose.

"Mentro?" Shakeera whispered.

The figure pulled back his dark eyes threatening to over fill with tears. There stood her older brother Mentro. His appearance hasn't changed at all from back then. The only difference was a little bit of gray hair was sprinkled within his hair. Shakeera placed her hands on the sides of his face. He gently rubbed her ears, chuckling softly.

"You finally grew into your ears." Mentro's voice cracked slightly.

"And you got your old man's hair in too." Shakeera giggled. Mentro hugged her tightly against his frame shaking.

"I'm... I'm so sorry Shakeera." Mentro cried.

"It was all my fault. That day you were kidnapped, I should have. If I were only stronger and faster...you." his voice cracked again as tears fell. Shakeera's ears drooped as her own tears fell.

"Oh Mentro...all this time you blame yourself. It wasn't your fault. It never was." Shakeera hugged Mentro tighter.

"Mentro? Was it Takeera?" A woman's voice came from the bushes.

A woman with light brown hair with cat ears came stumbling out of the plants. Shakeera's eyes widened as more tears fell, she held out her hand to the woman.

"Knala..." Shakeera whispered. Knala gasped running up to Shakeera and Mentro hugging them tightly.

"The whole gang is here now." Takeera squealed. Shakeera giggled, pulling away from her siblings walking over to Alcides.

"Everyone, this is Alcides. He's...me. Mate." Shakeera smiled up to him.

"Mate?" They exclaimed.

"Alcides this is my older brother Mentro, and this is my older sister Knala."

"Uhm hi there it's nice to meet you." Alcides said with a slight blush on his cheeks as Mentro and Knala walked up to him inspecting him from head to toe.

"He's human." Mentro said squaring up to him.

"Not that bad looking either." Knala said.

"He's also the prince of the west kingdom too." Shakeera added.

"Ooh fancy, we have royalty here." Knala stated.

"Even if he is royalty, he is still a man." Mentro said, looking Alcides in the eyes.

"You haven't DONE anything with my little sister have you?" Mentro growled. Alcides raised his hands up in defense.

"I'd never do anything like that to her I swear." Alcides stammered.

"Yeah, trust me, he is a gentleman compared to what the guards have done to me." Shakeera stated but mumbled the last part. Mentro jerked his head back baring his teeth.

"What was that!" Mentro yelled.

"That's in the past, there isn't any way anyone can change what happened back then. Right now," Shakeera took in a shaky breath.

"Right now, I want to see my mother." Shakeera rubbing her arm. Mentro and Knala nodded their heads as they started to walk through the trees leading Shakeera to their home. The home that she'd been away from for so long.

The group walked through the thick woods to come to a clearing with a man-made house that was built into the ground. A barn was behind it with a few fences around the land. A large garden of a variety of vegetables and fruits were growing next to the barn. As Shakeera walked up to the house flashbacks of her childhood flashed before her eyes. She made it to the front yard of the house seeing a small circle of rocks that had flowers planted within the circle. Some of the rocks were painted like children had done it. She knelt down gasping in surprise.

"I remember these, right Takeera? We painted these for mom on her birthday." Shakeera tenderly touched the faded painted rocks.

"Yeah, I remember that, but I remember we had a paint fight after we finished these." Takeera laughed. Shakeera's ears flipped back at a sound coming from behind her. The front door opened and a man's voice spoke.

"Oh Mentro, Knala, is everything alright? You just took off. I was worried something...had happened." The man paused for a moment as he looked at Shakeera who stood up looking at him. The man looked to be in his mid-forties with dark brown hair with peppered gray and white hairs throughout his head. He had his hair pulled back in a low ponytail. His eyes were a bright blue with a little dark shadow under his eyes. A brown beard filled his face that covered his lips.

"Dad?" Shakeera whispered softly. She walked up to the man looking up at him and her ears dropped down slightly.

"Shakeera? Is that you? You're still alive!" The man cupped her face looking deeply into her eyes thinking this was a dream.

"Yes dad... it's me." Shakeera's eyes started to water again. Her father choked a sob as he yanked her into his arms cupping the back of her head.

"Oh, my sweet girl. Oh! If this is a dream, please don't wake me up." He cried into her hair. Her siblings were hiding their tears at the happy reunion.

"Dad, I have someone I want you to meet. This is Alcides, the man who saved me from the battle arena, and my mate." Shakeera pulled back looking at Alcides.

Alcides blinked wide eyed, rubbing his hands on his pants before walking up to Shakeera and her father. He put his hand outwards with a small smile.

"It's nice to meet you sir, my name is Alcides Rockstin." Alcides waited for the man's response. The man looked at him wide eyed then cleared his throat grabbing Alcides's hand shaking it firmly.

"Nice to meet you Alcides, I'm Ben."

"Hey dad? Where's. Mom?" Shakeera peered up at him.

"Ah, she should be around here somewhere." Ben put his hands on his hips looking to the side of the house towards the garden.

"Ah here she comes." Ben stated.

Shakeera whipped her head to the direction her father was looking. A large feline the size of a pickup truck came walking around the corner with a basket full of vegetables from their garden in her mouth. She had light brown fur with blue speckled hairs scattered along her body.

Her amber eyes casted down looking at the bounty she had picked.

"Darling, I heard voices. Are the children, ok?" The feline looked up for a moment, her eyes widened big and her mouth opened dropping the basket scattering the produce on the ground.

"Sarah, we have a guest here to see you." Ben placed his hand on Shakeera's back.

Shakeera brought her hands up covering her mouth as tears fell from her eyes.

"Shakeera?" Sarah gasped.

She jolted forward running towards Shakeera who ran towards her. Sarah then morphed into a human looking being with the signature cat ears and tail. She had on a brown shirt and green pants. The two collided in a whirlwind of emotions as they spun around clutching each other crying.

"Oh mom! I'm sorry about everything! I'm sorry you got hurt because of me." Shakeera called out tears pouring down her cheeks. In her mother's form there was a huge scar that went from her neck that disappeared down her front.

"My sweet girl, you have nothing to be sorry about. I should be the one that should be apologizing to you. If I was stronger back when I tried to rescue you and not let my emotions overwhelm me you would have been home sooner." Sarah bawled.

"But look at you now, you've grown up so much. From what I have heard you've gotten strong too." Sarah pulled back, giving Shakeera a look over seeing how much she had grown.

"Hey mom, I have something to tell you. Well, more so to show you." Shakeera looked behind her to Alcides who looked awestruck.

"Mom, this is my mate, Alcides. Alcides, this is my mother, Sarah." Shakeera grabbed Alcides by the hand and pulled him towards Sarah.

Sarah's eyes grew big and her face lit up with happiness. Sarah walked up to Alcides examining him.

"He's human. You took after me with that." Sarah chuckled.

"Ah yes, I am human Mrs. Sarah." Alcides blushed slightly.

"You can just call me Sarah." She smiled.

"I see where she gets her beauty from." Alcides complimented.

"Oh now, flattery will get you everywhere. Are you hungry? Let's have some breakfast." Sarah laughed as she placed both of her hands on Alcides's and Shakeera's backs pushing them to the door. The family sat at the table enjoying their breakfast as Shakeera told them stories of her battles from the battle arena.

"With his last words being 'vile vermin', I yanked out his heart and won." Shakeera shoved her fist in the air.

"That's my girl!" Ben cheered.

"That was awesome, Shakeera! You've really learned a lot from being in that place." Mentro stated.

"I'm so proud of both of my girls. You two worked together to overcome one of the hardest things in life. I'm just so happy that you two are still alive." Sarah kissed Takeera and Shakeera on top of their heads.

"So, what's going to happen now with this battle arena? Since the head honcho is dead now, who's going to be in charge?" Ben asked.

"Well, I was thinking I could be in charge." Shakeera stated. Everyone's eyes were wide in shock but Alcides who just sat there smiling at her.

"But dear, why would you want to continue to stay there given your past there." Sarah asked, leaning on the table with her elbows.

"Well, yes. My past experience in that place wasn't the best. But now that Chase is gone, they need a leader. I know the ins and outs of that place. I'm going to change how the battle arena is going to be. For starters there will be no fighting to the death. There will be three rounds and whoever gets knocked down the most is out. There are a lot of half breeds out there that are homeless and not making ends meet. So, I'm going to help them by having them work in the battle arena. I will be holding classes to teach people how to defend themselves." Shakeera said right before taking a bite of bacon.

"You've really thought this through haven't you." Sarah commented.

"Yes, I have."

"Well, here's another question, since you've already done the mate ritual, will you have a human marriage ceremony?" Sarah asked locking eyes with both Alcides and Shakeera. The young couple blushed looking at each other then looked away in embarrassment.

"Well Sarah, I was thinking about having a ceremony. But I wasn't sure when would be a good time." Alcides cleared his throat.

"Yeah Ma, Alcides here is the prince of the west kingdom." Mentro said, picking his teeth with a toothpick. Sarah looked back at Alcides.

"You're the Prince of the west kingdom?" Sarah asked, lifting a brow.

"Yes Ma'am."

"What about your parents? What do they think about you two?"

"Well, they currently don't know about us I ran away from my kingdom because they were going to force me to marry the princess of the east. But I didn't have any romantic feelings for her. Something inside me told me that my true wife was out there somewhere. So, I left to look for her and that's where I met Shakeera." Alcides started grabbing Shakeera's hand under the table.

"I see." Sarah murmured.

"Oh mom, I forgot to tell you. Tonight, there is going to be a feast in celebration of me killing Chase. So, if everyone is up for it, you all can come and celebrate with us." Shakeera beamed.

"A celebration you say? What a coincidence." Sarah smiled a mischievous smile. Shakeera blinked then realized what her mother had in mind.

"Now mom, I know what you're thinking. There isn't any time for a wedding."

"Why not? You're going to have a celebration, why not have the wedding then?"

"We don't even have a priest or anything to do it so bad." Shakeera leaned back with her arms folded behind her head.

"Oh, that's right you didn't know your father could do it, he has the credentials to do it." Sarah placed her hand on Ben's shoulder.

"Then who is going to walk me down the aisle and hand me off?" Shakeera countered.

"I will." Mentro said firmly. Everyone turned their heads towards him.

"Really? Mentro? You'll walk me down the aisle?" Shakeera asked.

"Yeah, it's my duty Isn't it? As the older brother I am the one that has to protect you. But now that you have your mate now, I have to give that duty to him." Mentro nodded his head towards Alcides.

Alcides looked at Mentro seeing him more than just her older brother. But a man who had a large boulder of guilt that had weighed him down for so long. He lost his little sister back then and now he is going to lose his sister once again. He has barely just got her back.

"Thank you, Mentro, that means a lot to me." Shakeera smiled at Mentro.

15

Alcides and Mentro started their trip back to the battle arena to tell Zeek about the wedding. Alcides glanced at Mentro who looked like he was in his own little world. Mentro having an internal battle raging in side him. His features went from happy to a pained look in a split second. Alcides didn't really know what Mentro was going through because he was an only child. Alcides looked ahead seeing a Peacockian pair walking towards them.

"Oh hey!" Alcides called out waving at them. They waved back smiling.

"Hey, can you tell Zeek to meet us at the main gate? We have some big news to tell him." Alcides beamed.

"Yes!" They chimed together and turned around running back to where they were coming from.

"Who were they?" Mentro asked as they started to walk again.

"They are a part of a village of Peacockians that Shakeera and I met on our way to my kingdom. They helped us out and let us stay with them. They helped Shakeera come out of her shell a little too. It's kinda funny, they were having a festival for the celebration. Apparently, Shakeera had killed a very bad person from their village and so they have a big festival celebrating his death."

"Wow really?" Mentro asked in awe.

"Yeah. Zeek is the one that is the head of the village in a way. His wife helped Shakeera find her 'inner female' if you will." Alcides did air quotes with his hands.

Mentro looked confused trying to comprehend what Alcides was saying. To Mentro, Shakeera was always his little sister, a female, feminine.

"Ah, let me try to explain it another way. The battle arena is a very male dominant sport and place. So, she was forced into male activities. The winner of each battle gets to enjoy a session with the beauties." Alcides explained. It took Mentro a few seconds to connect the dots then his eyes widened as big as saucer plates. He shook his head violently trying to keep the images of his little sister doing the deed with other females.

"I kinda knew she wasn't that girly to begin with but to know she did those...kind of things." Mentro tried his best to get his words out but couldn't.

"Unreal right?" Alcides stated. Mentro looked back at Alcides.

"Knowing your kid sister has been doing god knows what with god knows who." Alcides continued.

Mentro stopped dead in his tracks. His whole world was crashing around him, everything he knew, everything he wanted to do to protect his sister just burned up in his face. Alcides stopped seeing the state of how Mentro looked. He walked to him, placing his hands on Mentro's shoulders making him look up.

"With all that said she still fought strong. She remembered all the lessons that you and everyone else in your family taught her. Shakeera survived ten long traumatic years in that hellhole because of you Mentro. You can't change what happened in the past, all you can do is move on and be there for her in her future." Alcides stated, looking Mentro in the eyes.

"Even if Shakeera and I are mates and we are doing a human marriage, I'm not going to keep you and her apart. I promise you that." Alcides patted Mentro's shoulder and started walking again.

A few miles from the border of the east kingdom and Zira a carriage being pulled by centaur half breeds. The king and queen of the West was returning from a visit from the East. The queen sighed in defeat.

"Well, I'm glad that the princess of the East wasn't to hurt about the news." The queen stated.

"Yes, it is a good thing, poor thing didn't seem to be bothered by it. She just shrugged her shoulders." The king was pushing buttons on a remote control changing the channel on the screen in front of them.

"I'm still worried about Alcides, after his disappearance, I don't know where that boy is. Is he safe? Is he even alive?" The queen stressed, placing a hand over her chest trying to calm herself down.

"I'm sure he is fine dear; we've taught that boy everything he knows." The king trailed off as he stopped at a channel advertising the battle arena. At that moment Alcides face was smack dab in the middle of the screen. The king shook his head rubbing his eyes in disbelief. Reaching a hand over he tapped on the queen's knee gently.

"What is it?" The queen asked.

"I found our son." The king pointed at the screen. The queen looked at the screen and gasped.

"Driver!" The king called out.

"Yes sir!" The driver called back.

"Go to this Zira there is something important there we need to take care of." The king stated.

"Yes sir." The driver whipped the reins making the half breeds run faster.

Alcides and Mentro cleared the forest, seeing the walls of Zira and the big sign up above the gate. Mentro only has been to Zira a handful of times just to help Takeera to get in to hide when she would go and see Shakeera. He would come here to sell some of his family's crops from time to time. He didn't like how crowded it was when he came there. As they walked through the gates they were greeted with a very loud and proud Peacockian strutting his stuff as he approached them.

"Ah Alcides I came as you requested. What is it you need?" Zeek asked.

"Well, there is a change of plans, well more so an addition to it." Alcides stated.

"Oh? Do tell." Zeek said, leaning closer.

"In addition to the feast there is going to be a wedding. Shakeera's and I's wedding to be exact." Alcides said with a blush on his cheeks. Zeek let out a loud call that got everyone's attention.

"Excellent news indeed! Attention everyone! In addition to the feast there will be a wedding!

For your champion Shakeera and this man right here! Everyone let's get this wedding started!" Zeek called out wrapping his arm around Alcides shoulder.

Everyone in the marketplace gasped and cheered while doing their part in getting the wedding ready. Just as they started to walk towards the battle arena the ground shook under them drawing their attention back to the gate where a large dust cloud was barreling towards them. Once the rumbling of the ground had stopped and the dust had cleared a carriage was revealed.

"Who's that?" Mentro asked. Alcides stood there silently not knowing what to say. The carriage's doors opened and two figures came out looking over at Mentro and Alcides. Alcides' whole body went rigid after recognizing the two people who had stepped out.

"They, they are my parents." Alcides stated.

"Wait, they're your parents?" Mentro asked, looking from Alcides to the carriage then back to Alcides.

The man that had stepped out first was helping the woman out of the carriage. The woman looked in Alcides, she peered at him for a few seconds then she gasped shifting on her feet fanning herself. She let out a loud 'woo' noise then shuffled her feet then turned into a power walk engulfing Alcides in her arms.

"Oh! Oh! My dear son Alcides! Where have you been? I was so worried about you! I thought you were dead! Oh!" She called out tears fell from her eyes. She pulled back, placing her hands on either side of his face squishing his cheeks together while examining him from head to toe.

"What happened to your hair? You cut it? Your beautiful hair!" She exclaimed once more pulling him close burying his face into her large bosom. The man approached them, saving his son from suffocation.

"Yes, son we both have been worried sick about you. We just left the East kingdom after talking with the king and queen about your disappearance. Now tell us what's going on here?" The man looked at Alcides sternly.

"Mom, Dad, I uhh here's the thing- "Alcides started to say but was interrupted by Zeek who came back to the group.

"What's the hold up? Come now come now! We have a wedding to get set up." Zeek called out fanning his tail feathers again while turning on his heels walking away.

"Wedding? What wedding?" Alcide's mother looked confused. Zeek turned on his heels again sashaying back to them.

"Why yes, a wedding! For our Alcides here. He's getting married." Zeek sang out. Both of Alcides' parents looked at Alcides in confusion.

"So, you're telling us that instead of you marrying the princess of the east you ran away to get married to some other girl?" Alcides's father asked.

"I, uh.... yes, it's hard to explain." Alcides said, rubbing his neck nervously. "Follow me and I will do my best to explain ok?" Alcides motioned for them to follow.

"For a good portion of my life I've felt like something was telling me to go find my true one love, my mate." Alcides continued.

"Mate?" His parents said in unison.

"Yes, when you told me I was supposed to marry the princess of the east I couldn't wrap my mind around it. Even when we did the meet and greet. My heart didn't pound in my chest like it should have. When I looked at the princess, I could see she wasn't too keen on it either. Day after day I felt this kind of pull that kept making me want to leave our kingdom to find my true love. Like a little voice telling me 'Come and find me'. It grew more and more intense until I couldn't take it anymore. So, I set out on a journey to find my mate, my wife and that's where I met Shakeera."

"Shakeera? This girl. You say she is your true love?" His father asked as they walked through the gate of the battle arena. His mother looked around seeing posters and screens with a girl with cat ears in fighting poses or attacking some monster. She then saw the name Shakeera on a screen she then stopped dead in her tracks staring at the screen.

"Alcides, dear, is this the Shakeera girl that you are going to be married to?" Alcides' mother pointed at the screen that hung over their heads. Alcides stopped glancing up at the screen. The corner of his mouth pulled up into a cute smile.

"Yes, that is my Shakeera." Alcides stated.

"But she is clearly a- "She started but Alcides cut her off.

"A half breeds? Yes. I am aware she is a half breed mother. To be frank, why does it matter? She didn't have a choice on how she was born or what side of the population she was going to be on." Alcides turned to face his parents holding his head high then he pointed to his mate's mark on his neck.

"Shakeera and I are already mates on her terms. This wedding is a formality for the human side of our lives." There was a moment of silence between Alcides and his parents. His parents looked at one another then nodded.

"Alright son, if this is what you want, we approve. Under one condition once everything is done here." His mother waved her hand around to indicate this wedding.

"You will come back home and we will have our own wedding to show our people of our kingdom that their prince has found his true love deal?" His mother asked. Alcide's eyes lit up with joy as he nodded his head.

"Thank you, mom, dad, really you both will love her." Alcides said with excitement. His parents chuckled at his statement. The king placed his hand on his wife's shoulder getting her attention.

"My dear, would you help the people here with the decorations and such? I'm going to take our son to the market here to find him a good outfit for his wedding."

"Yes darling, see you both back here soon." The queen smiled waving at both of them then starting to follow Zeek into the battle arena.

Alcides and his father turned and started to walk back out of the gates to the marketplace.

They stopped at several stalls to find some nice black dress shoes. The next stall they went to was selling high end clothing. Alcides stood in a makeshift changing room to get fitted for his wedding suit.

"Now son there is something I want to discuss with you." The king cleared his throat.

"I have a feeling I know what you want to talk about, father."

"It's nothing to worry about right at this moment. But your mother and I won't be alive forever. Someday you will have to become king. With you already having a wife now you have your queen too." The king said, pointing out a nice dark blue suit and pants combo. Alcides sighed, rolling his eyes as he looked up at the ceiling of the tent.

"But father, I have no desire to be king. I also don't think Shakeera would want to be queen either. I just want to help people in the kingdoms and around the world. Making all species united and not divided." Alcides stated.

"That is quite a dream you have. I admire your courage my son. Once you become king you will be able to do anything you want. But you will have to be able to rule over your own kingdom. To take care of the people of your land." The king stated

"Just give me some time to think about it and talk with Shakeera alright?" Alcides pleaded.

"Alright son. This is your big day after all. Oh, almost forgot, I will be right back." The King pardoned himself as he left the tent.

Ten minutes had passed and the King had returned with a small box in his hand. Alcides had finished getting dressed, he turned to see his father had returned. His father held out the box handing it to Alcides.

"We can't forget the rings." His father pointed to the box. Alcides opened the box to reveal one silver band and a smaller silver band with black onyx vines etched into the medal.

"They're perfect father, thank you." Alcides tucked the box away in his jacket pocket.

After paying the merchant Alcides and his father walked through the marketplace when all of a sudden Alcides heard his name being called.

He turned around to see Takeera and her sister Knala and their father walking up to them.

"Wow Al you look really handsome in that outfit. Takeera stated giving him a look over.

"Well thank you Takeera. Dad this is Shakeera's family. This is Takeera, Shakeera's twin sister. This is Knala their older sister and this is Ben, their father. He is going to be doing the ceremony. Everyone this is my father, the king of the west." Alcides introduced everyone.

"Nice to meet you all. So, who's going to be the flower girl and the maid of honor?" The king asked.

"Well, I could be the maid of honor since I'm her older sister." Knala said.

"I'll be the flower girl!" Takeera beamed.

"Alright sounds like a plan. Son if you will, go check on your mother while I get the girls their outfits." The king smiled placing his hands on Takeera's and Knala's shoulder.

"Ok dad just doesn't go overboard, ok?" Alcides asked as he walked alongside Shakeera's father. Ben glanced at Alcides from the corner of his eye seeing that Alcides was nervous.

"Uhh...Ben? May I ask you a question?" Alcides asked.

"Sure, go on ahead." Ben smiled, knowing what he was going to ask.

"Were you nervous too? I mean, when you married Sarah?" Alcides asked with a slight blush on his cheeks. He was taken back when Ben let out a soft chuckle.

"I'm sorry for the laugh. But yes, I was quite nervous on our wedding day. With the whole human and demon dynamics, her parents weren't too keen on the whole engagement all together. My parents died when I was a teenager, but before they passed, they were open minded. Sarah being a demon and all I knew that my mere human life span wouldn't be up to par with hers. She will outlive me by a long shot. But that day, on our wedding day It felt like my heart was going to leap out of my throat. I knew that after that moment I knew our lives would be a struggle because our kids would be half breeds. But you know what, I didn't care. I loved Sarah with all my heart. I wouldn't change a thing even if I could." Ben smiled up at the sky. Ben then looked at Alcides placing a hand on his shoulder reassuringly.

"You don't have to worry. Love will overcome everything." Ben stated.

"Thank you, sir." Alcides smiled as they walked through the entrance of the battle arena. As they passed the threshold his eyes widened in amazement. The once death place of a battle arena that took lives left and right was now a place that looked like it should be in a fairy tale. White banners were streamed across the whole area. White and gold flowers were placed along the ring of the arena. A red strip of carpet was making a path to the altar. Alcides mother comes walking to Alcides and Ben fanning herself her cheeks red from all the work she did.

"Oh, hello Alcides darling what do you think?" She gestured around them.

"Mom this is amazing you did a great job. Oh, this is Ben, Shakeera's father. He will be helping with the wedding." Alcides introduced

Ben. Ben nodded his head, taking her hand tenderly.

"A pleasure to meet you Madam."

"Likewise." The queen nodded. She turned to Alcides cupping his face in her hands. Tears threatened to fall as she looked at her son.

"Oh, my boy is getting married, I'm so happy for you." The queen bawled.

"Now mom if you keep crying like this I'm going to start crying and it will not end well." Alcides smiled at his mother who nodded her head.

Alcides took in his surroundings smiling big knowing in just a few hours he and Shakeera will be getting married.

16

The Wedding

Hours passed until the time of the wedding came. The seats were all being filled till there were no more seats to be filled. There were crowds outside the battle arena watching the screens waiting for the big wedding to start. A group of Peacockians stood off to the side of the altar singing a nice slow song. Ben stood at the altar motioning for the males to start singing a new tune. Everyone turned their attention to the main entrance where Alcides and his mother stood side by side, arms linked together. They started to take their steps down the aisle with Alcides' father in tow. When they arrived at the front part of the altar, Alcides led his mother and father to their seats. Alcides walked up to the small staged area of the altar glancing back at his parents who beamed happily at him. Ben singled for the group to sing in unison as the wedding was about to start.

Outside at the entrance of the battle arena Sarah walked out of the forest in her demon form with Shakeera on her back with Takeera and Knala walking beside her. The girls could see the battle arena all lit up and a line of people making an aisle for the important bride. Sarah lowered herself to the ground helping Shakeera to the ground safely then transformed to her humanoid form.

"Ok my beautiful daughters, let's get in line. Takeera, you take the lead, then it will be Knala and me then the woman of the hour, Shakeera. Mentro will walk you down the aisle." Sarah turned around cupping Shakeera's cheeks gently kissing the top of her head.

Sarah turned back around, stopping mid step, her ears flicking forward as she heard something. She shook her head dismissing the feeling something was going to happen. The crowd of people cheered as the ladies approached the battle arena. Mentro briskly walked up to the group looking like he had been running a marathon.

"Wow everyone looks beautiful." Mentro smiled seeing how everyone was dressed.

Takeera had a pale-yellow dress with little flowers around the edges of her dress. Knala wore a similar dress but with darker designs. Sarah wore a long sleeved white and yellow dress. Takeera held her head high, placing a smile that could brighten any room. She started to walk down the aisle tossing the basket full of flowers to the ground. Sarah stepped up to stand next to Knala linking their arms together.

"Let's go my dear." Sarah smiled at her daughter then took her steps down the aisle a few feet from Takeera.

Shakeera stepped up to Mentro clutching the flower bouquet tightly in her hands as she watched her mom and sisters parading down the aisle. Mentro could see how nervous his little sister was. He offered his elbow to her, giving her the best big brother smile he could muster. Shakeera smiled up at him then placed her forehead on his shoulder.

"I'm one of the toughest half breeds in the whole area, I've killed every human and demon that were thrown at me. But, here I am. Afraid to step foot into this place to get married to a man I love." Shakeera murmured.

"You love him, don't you?" Mentro asked.

"What?"

"I asked if you loved him or not?" Mentro replied, looking down at her.

"Well, yes I do love him."

"And he clearly loves you, no man would do what he has done if he didn't love you." Mentro placed his free hand on hers.

"It's normal for anyone to be nervous on a big day like today. Here I am your older brother, just about to hand my baby sister over to a man that I just met. You're being taken away from me again, just like before when you were taken away that day." Mentro clutched Shakeera's hand tightly.

"Mentro," Shakeera sighed looking up at him, tears threatening to fall.

"I'm not being taken away; you and I both know Alcides will take care of me. Now let's get this all done so I can take this damn dress off." Both Shakeera and Mentro laughed as they took their steps down the aisle.

Shakeera and Mentro walked side by side down the aisle. Everyone in their seats stood up gasping in awe seeing Shakeera dressed so beautifully. Shakeera looked around seeing all of the guests that had attended. They weren't here to watch her fight but to start a new chapter in life. Shakeera finally spotted the big reason why she was here today. There stood Alcides, hands clasped behind his back. Their eyes locked for a moment; Shakeera's eyes widened as her chest grew tight. Every step they took her heart would beat faster and faster. It felt like it was an eternity walking down that aisle. Mentro stopped right before the altar looking down to Shakeera seeing that she wasn't all there at the moment. He shifted his weight slightly, nudging her gently. Shakeera jerked out of her fantasy world. Her head snapped to the side as something caught her attention. Her ears flicked in every direction trying to analyze what was going on. A shiver went through her spine.

"You, ok? What's wrong?" Mentro whispered to Shakeera. She shook her head smiling at him.

"Nothing it's nothing, sorry." Shakeera waved it off.

"Now who is giving the bride away?" Ben cleared his throat before asking the question. Mentro collected himself standing straight.

"I am." Mentro said while taking Shakeera's hand in his. He gently placed hers onto Alcides with his own covering theirs. He looked Alcides in the eyes.

"I Mentro, Shakeera's older brother is giving my little sister to you." Mentro said loudly then he leaned closer to Alcides lowering his voice so just Alcides and him could hear it.

"If you do anything to hurt her emotionally or physically, I will make your death look like an accident." Mentro said, not losing eye contact as he reluctantly lifted his hands from their joint ones. He nodded his head towards them walking to his mother sitting next to her.

"We are gathered here today to join these two souls in holy matrimony..." Ben started the ceremony.

The ceremony went off without a hitch, everyone's spirits were high. Outside the battle arena a few miles away was a landfill full of bodies of the victims from the many fights. The top of the mound of body parts and mush, something started to stir. Something was sloshing around left and right. There was a low rumble heard as a bubble serviced it started to inflate. Bigger and bigger it went until it stretched thin and popped splattering everywhere. The mound started to shake and a large ball flew out of the pile. Chase's head went soaring into the sky making a beeline to the battle arena.

"If anyone has an objection to why these two cannot be married let them speak now or forever hold their peace." Ben stated as there was a moment of silence. Just as Ben was about to finish the ceremony by saying,

"As the power vested in me, I pronounce you husband and wife you may kiss the bride- "In the middle of his sentence as Chase's roaring voice came booming from above the battle arena.

Shakeera heard Chase's voice; her head shot up. Seeing that grotesque monstrous face zooming his way down to them her ears flicked back.

"You…. may…. kiss…the.br- "Shakeera reached forward gently grabbing the back of Alcides head pulling him towards her.

Alcides was oblivious of what was going on around him. One moment he was staring at Shakeera in her beautiful wedding dress, her bright blue eyes staring right back at him. He didn't notice that Shakeera had cupped the back of his head and started to pull him close to her face. She rolled them over so she was above him, dipping him down like how they first met. Alcides barely registered the position that he was in until he saw Chase's head flying right at him. His eyes widened but his vision was blocked by Shakeera's face obscuring his line of vision. She closed her eyes pressing their lips together as she shot her other arm in the air with her palm facing the sky. Her vine shot out of her palm rocketing right to Chase's head creating an explosion in the sky.

On that day, the two souls became one.

About the Author

Aris Bolvi was always a sucker for anything unique. Let it be mythical or supernatural, anything that wasn't normal. Alongside the love of being different she loves romance. Aris was born in Maryland. Her family then moved to Thailand due to her father's line of work. Living there for four years, she had experienced a lot from living there that not alot of girls her age would have gone through. Her family finally settled down in Arizona where she had started her journey in writing. Aris started to venture into the writing world by writing fanfiction. The more she wrote fanfiction, the more she wanted to create her own world with her own characters. Testing the waters of creating her own unique universe she started to role play as her characters on a website called Bebo. "The Tragic Tale of a Half breed" is a product from that adventure. Her upcoming books are also from her time on Bebo.